PHELIM O'TOOLE'S COURTSHIP

AND OTHER STORIES

MERCIER IRISH CLASSICS
Traits & Stories of the Irish Peasantry, Volume III

PHELIM O'TOOLE'S COURTSHIP

and other stories

by

WILLIAM CARLETON

With an Introduction by
MAURICE HARMON

THE MERCIER PRESS
Cork and Dublin

THE MERCIER PRESS LIMITED
4 Bridge Street, Cork
25 Lower Abbey Street, Dublin 1

PHELIM O'TOOLE'S COURTSHIP
AND OTHER STORIES

ISBN 0 85342 341 5

This is Volume 3 of a series of eight volumes containing a complete and unabridged edition of William Carleton's *Traits & Stories of the Irish Peasantry*

Printed in Ireland by
the Leinster Leader Limited

CONTENTS

INTRODUCTION TO VOLUME THREE

In "Phelim O'Toole's Courtship" we find Carleton working in that ironic and mocking manner already used to great effect in "Denis O'Shaughnessy Going to Maynooth". Here, too, comic exaggeration is used to great effect in presenting the figure of Phelim O'Toole, the bold irresponsible Irish lad, a local hero, his parents's pride and product of his upbringing. The story moves through a series of deceptions and intrigues and might be seen as complementary to Maria Edgeworth's *Castle Rackrent*, where an irresponsible way of life is also projected in a series of representative incidents.

Carleton has never been examined in the light of those folk tale elements that he encountered so intimately in his own locality and heard from his storytelling father, but they are clearly present in "The Three Tasks" and in the narrative conventions followed in "Phelim O'Toole's Courtship". Frank O'Connor, making a distinction between the literary story and the oral tale, pointed out that the latter has a preference for marvels and requires an audience. The literary story implies an audience and its form is determined only by its own material and not at all by the presence of an audience, real or imaginary. The point is particularly relevant for the story of Phelim O'Toole and for "The Three Tasks". Both have comic exaggeration, fantastic events and the unexpected. In Phelim's case it is also evident that he is in essence a folk hero and has those qualities admired by the folk imagination which have almost nothing to do with conventional morality or social values that obtain in urban society.

"The Three Tasks" bears the direct influence of the oral tradition, in particular the Tyrone folktale about Jack and the Black

Horse, but the tale in which a hero is faced with three impossible tasks at the risk of his own death is found in innumerable forms in the international folktale. Jack Magennis's encounter with the Dark Man and his enigmatic dog and his Faustian bargain in an Irish bog is presented with skill and irony. And Jack's ability to compliment the lady in the Dark Man's castle resembles Phelim's various scenes of courtship. Their escape from the castle is right out of the folktale tradition. In the version of the story of Jack and the Black Horse taken down in Tyrone in 1908, the Black Horse, who is a beautiful prince in disguise, advises Jack: "look in my right ear now and see do you see anything in it".

"I see a drop of water in it," says Jack.

"Throw it behind you," say the Black Horse, "and wish for an ocean behind you and a plain road before you."

". . . and a wide sea spread itself behind them. When the pursuing giants came the length of it they made three horses of themselves and thought to drink the water dry."

"An Essay on Irish Swearing", as Thomas Flanagan says in *The Irish Novelists 1800-1850* is a bitter and caustic satire on those writers of the *Blackwoods* school who professed to find "Paddy" a compound of wit and murder, too innocent in his violence to deserve full moral censure. "But it is also an angry, self-despising attack upon his own people, who had chosen sound rather than sense. The "poetic" quality of peasant speech could make a chivalric hero of "the poor boy who perhaps only burnt a family in their beds." The rich honey of its rhetoric could coat the most savage and degenerate of crimes. Half a century before John Synge put his ear to a Wicklow floor to catch the talk of servant girls, Carleton had caught every turn and nuance of Irish speech. Unlike Synge, he judged, moralized, interrupted himself with sermons and imprecations, for he was a writer by nature far more conscious of the moral source and moral consequences of language.

PHELIM O'TOOLE'S COURTSHIP

PHELIM O'TOOLE, who had the honour of being that interesting personage, an only son, was heir to a snug estate of half an acre, which had been the family patrimony since the time of his grandfather, Tyrrell O'Toole, who won it from the *Sassenach* at the point of his reaping-hook, during a descent once made upon England by a body of *spalpeens*, in the month of August. This resolute little band was led on by Tyrrell, who, having secured about eight guineas by the excursion, returned to his own country with a coarse linen travelling-bag slung across his shoulder, a new hat in one hand, and a staff in the other. On reaching once more his native village of Teernarogarth, he immediately took half an acre, for which he paid a moderate rent in the shape of daily labour as a cottar. On this he resided until death, after which event he was succeeded by his son, Larry O'Toole, the father of the "purty boy" who is about to shine in the following pages.

Phelim's father and mother had been married near seven years without the happiness of a family. This to both was a great affliction. Sheelah O'Toole was melancholy from night to morning, and Larry was melancholy from morning to night. Their cottage was silent and solitary; the floor and furniture had not the appearance of any cottage in which Irish children are wont to amuse themselves. When they rose in the morning a miserable stillness prevailed around them; young voices were not heard—laughing eyes turned not on their parents—the melody of angry squabbles, as the urchins, in their parents' fancy, cuffed and scratched each other—half or wholly naked among the ashes in the morning, soothed not the yearning hearts of Larry and his wife. No, no; there was none of this. Morning passed in a quietness hard to be borne; noon arrived, but the dismal, dreary sense of childlessness hung upon the house of their hearts; night again returned, only to add its darkness to that which overshadowed the sorrowful spirits of this disconsolate couple.

For the first two or three years they bore this privation with a strong confidence that it would not last. The heart, however, sometimes becomes tired of hoping, or unable to bear the burden of expectation, which time only renders heavier. They first began to fret and pine, then to murmur, and finally to recriminate.

Sheelah wished for children, "to have the crathurs to spake to," she said, "and comfort us when we'd get ould an' helpless."

Larry cared not, provided they had a son to inherit the "half acre." This was the burden of his wishes, for in all their altercations his closing observation usually was, "Well, but what's to become of the half acre?"

"What's to become of the half acre? *Arrah*, what do I care for the half acre? It's not that you ought to be thinkin' of, but the dismal poor house we have, wid not the laugh or schreech of a single *pastiah* in it from year's end to year's end."

"Well, Sheelah?"

"Well yourself, Larry? To the *diouol* I pitch your half acre, man."

"To the *diouol* you pitch—What do you fly at me for?"

"Who's flyin' at you? They'd have little tow on their rock that ud fly at you."

"You are flyin' at me; an' only you have a hard face you wouldn't do it."

"A hard face! Indeed it's well come over wid us, to be tould that by the likes o' you—ha!"

"No matther for that! You had bether keep a soft tongue in your head, an' a civil one, in the manetime. Why did the divil timpt you to take a fancy to me at all?"

"That's it—throw the *grah* an' love I once had for you in my teeth now. It's a manly thing for you to do, an' you may be proud of it. Dear knows it would be bether for me I had fell in consate wid any face but yours."

"I wish to goodness you had! I wouldn't be as I am to-day. There's that half acre——"

"To the *diouol*, I say, I pitch yourself an' your half acre!

2

Why do you be comin' acrass me wid your half acre? Eh? Why do you?"

"Come, now; don't be puttin' your hands agin your sides an' waggin' your impty head at me, like a rockin' stone."

"An' why do you be aggravatin' at me wid your half acre?"

"Bekase I have a good right to do it. What'll become of it when I d——"

"That for you an' it, you poor excuse!"

"When I di——"

"That for you an' it, I say! That for you an' it, you atomy!"

"What will become of my half acre when I die? Did you hear that?"

"You ought to think of what'll become of yourself when you die—that's what you ought to think of; but little it throubles you, you sinful reprobate! Sure, the neighbours despises you."

"That's a falsity. But they know the life I lade wid you. The edge of your tongue's well known. They pity me for bein' joined to the likes of you. Your bad tongue's all you're good for."

"Aren't you afeard to be flyin' in the face o' Providence the way you are? an' to be ladin' me sich a heart-scalded life for no rason?"

"It's your own story you're tellin'. Sure, I haven't a day's pace wid you, or ever had these three years. But wait till next harvest, an' if I'm spared I'll go to England. Whin I do, I've a consate in my head that you'll never see my face agin."

"Oh, you know that's an' ould story wid you. Many a time you threatened us wid that afore. Who knows but you'd be dhrownded on your way, an' thin we'd get another husband."

"An' be these blessed tongs I'll do it afore I'm much ouldher!"

"An' lave me here to starve an' sthruggle by myself! Desart me like a villain, to poverty an' hardship! Marciful Mother of Heaven, look down upon me this day! but I'm the ill-thrated an' ill-used poor crathur, by a man that I don't, an' never did, desarve it from! An' all in regard that that 'half acre' must go to strangers! Och! oh!"

3

"Ay! now take to the cryin'—do; rock yourself over the ashes, an' wipe your eyes wid the corner of your apron; but I say agin, what's to become of the half acre?"

"Oh, God forgive you, Larry! That's the worst I say to you, you poor half-dead blackguard!"

"Why do you massacray me wid your tongue as you do?"

"Go an—go an. I won't make you an answer, you atomy! That's what I'll do. The heavens above turn your heart this day, and give me strinth to bear my throubles an' heart-burnin', sweet Queen o' Consolation! Or take me into the arms of Parodies, sooner nor be as I am, wid a poor baste of a villain, that I never turn my tongue on, barrin' to tell him the kind of a man he is, the blackguard!"

"You're betther than you desarve to be!"

To this Sheelah made no further reply; on the contrary, she sat smoking her pipe with a significant silence, that was only broken by an occasional groan, an ejaculation, or a singularly devout upturning of the eyes to heaven, accompanied by a shake of the head, at once condemnatory and philosophical, indicative of her dissent from what he said, as well as of her patience in bearing it.

Larry, however, usually proceeded to combat all her gestures by *viva voce* argument: for every shake of her head he had an appropriate answer, but without being able to move her from the obstinate silence she maintained. Having thus the field to himself, and feeling rather annoyed by the want of an antagonist, he argued on in the same form of dispute; whilst she, after first calming her own spirit by the composing effects of the pipe, usually cut him short with—

"Here, take a blast o' this; maybe it'll settle you."

This was received in silence. The good man smoked on, and every puff appeared as an evaporation of his anger. In due time he was as placid as herself; drew his breath in a grave, composed manner; laid his pipe quietly on the hob, and went about his business as if nothing had occurred between them.

These bickerings were strictly private, with the exception of some disclosures made to Sheelah's mother and sisters. Even these were thrown out rather as insinuations that all was not right, than as direct assertions that they lived unhappily. Before strangers they were perfect turtles.

4

Larry, according to the notices of his life furnished by Sheelah, was "as good a husband as ever broke the world's bread;" and Sheelah "was as good a poor man's wife as ever threw a gown over her shoulders." Notwithstanding all this caution, their little quarrels took wind, their unhappiness became known. Larry, in consequence of a failing he had, was the cause of this. He happened to be one of those men who can conceal nothing when in a state of intoxication. Whenever he indulged in liquor too freely, the veil which discretion had drawn over their recriminations was put aside, and a dolorous history of their weaknesses, doubts, hopes, and wishes most unscrupulously given to every person on whom the complainant could fasten. When sober he had no recollection of this, so that many a conversation of cross-purposes took place between him and his neighbours with reference to the state of his domestic inquietude and their want of children.

One day a poor mendicant came in at dinner-hour, and stood as if to solicit alms. It is customary in Ireland when any person of that description appears during meal-times, to make him wait until the meal is over, after which he is supplied with the fragments. No sooner had the *boccagh*—as a certain class of beggars is termed—advanced past the jamb than he was desired to sit until the dinner should be concluded. Meantime, with the tact of an adept in his calling, he began to ingratiate himself with Larry and his wife; and after sounding the simple couple upon their private history, he discovered that want of children was the occasion of their unhappiness.

"Well, good people," said the pilgrim, after listening to a dismal story on the subject, "don't be cast down, sure, whether or not. There's a holy well that I can direct yees to in the county ——. Any one, wid trust in the saint that's over it, who'll make a pilgrimage to it on the patthern day, won't be the worse for it. When you go there," he added, "jist turn to a lucky stone that's at the side of the well, say a rosary before it, and at the end of every dicken (decade) kiss it once, ache of you. Then you're to go round the well nine times upon your bare knees, sayin' your pathers and aves all the time. When that's over, lave a ribbon or a bit of your dress behind you, or somethin' by way of an offerin', thin go

5

into a tent an' refresh yourselves, an', for thát matther, take a dance or two ; come home, live happily, an' trust to the holy saint for the rest."

A gleam of newly awakened hope might be discovered lurking in the eyes of this simple pair, who felt those natural yearnings of heart incident to such as are without offspring.

They looked forward with deep anxiety to the anniversary of the patron saint ; and when it arrived, none certainly who attended it felt a more absorbing interest in the success of the pilgrimage than they did.

The days on which these pilgrimages are performed at such places are called pattern or patron days. The journey to holy wells or holy lakes is termed a pilgrimage, or more commonly a station. It is sometimes enjoined by the priest as an act of penance, and sometimes undertaken voluntarily as a devotional work of great merit in the sight of God. The crowds in many places amount to from five hundred to a thousand, and often to two, three, four, or ten thousand people.

These stations have, for the most part, been placed in situations remarkable for wild and savage grandeur, or for soft, exquisite, and generally solitary beauty. They may be found on the high and rugged mountain-top, or sunk in the bottom of some still and lonely glen, far removed from the ceaseless din of the world. Immediately beside them, or close in their vicinity, stand the ruins of, probably, a picturesque old abbey, or perhaps a modern chapel. The appearance of these grey, ivy-covered walls is strongly calculated to stir up in the minds of the people the memory of bygone times, when their religion, with its imposing solemnities, was the religion of the land.

Let the reader, in order to understand the situation of the place we are describing, imagine to himself a stupendous cliff overhanging a green glen, into which tumbles a silver stream down a height of two or three hundred feet. At the bottom of this rock, a few yards from the basin formed by the cascade, in a sunless nook, was a well of cool, delicious water. This was the "holy well," out of which issued a slender stream that joined the rivulet formed by the cascade. On the shrubs which grew out of the crag-cliffs around it might be seen innumerable rags bleached by the weather out of their original colour, small wooden crosses, locks of human hair, buttons, and other substitutes for property—poverty allowing the people to offer it only by fictitious emblems. Lower down in the glen, on the river's bank, was a smooth green, admirably adapted for the dance, which, notwithstanding the religious rites, is the heart and soul of a patron.

On that morning a vast influx of persons, male and female, old and young, married and single, crowded eagerly towards the well. Among them might be noticed the blind, the lame, the paralytic, and such as were afflicted with various other diseases; nor were those good men who had no offspring to be omitted. The mendicant, the pilgrim, the *boccagh*, together with every other description of impostors remarkable for attending such places, were the first on the ground, all busy in their respective vocations. The highways, the fields, and the *boreens*, or bridle-roads, were filled with living streams of people pressing forward to this great scene of fun and religion. The devotees could in general be distinguished from the country folks by their pharisaical and penitential visages, as well as by their not wearing shoes, for the stations to such places were formerly made with bare feet—most persons now, however, content themselves with stripping off their shoes and stockings on coming within the precincts of the holy ground. Human beings are not the only description of animals that perform pilgrimages to holy wells and blessed lakes. Cows, horses, and sheep are made to go through their duties, either by way of prevention or cure of the diseases incident to them. This is not to be wondered at when it is known that every domestic animal has its patron saint, to whom its owner may at any time pray on its behalf.

When the crowd was collected, nothing in the shape of an assembly could surpass it in the originality of its appearance. In the glen were constructed a number of tents, where whisky and refreshments might be had in abundance. Every tent had a fiddler or a piper; many two of them. From the top of a pole that ran up from the roof of each tent was suspended the symbol by which the owner of it was known by his friends and acquaintances. Here swung a salt herring or a turf, there a shillelah, in a third place a shoe, in a fourth place a wisp of hay, in a fifth an old hat, and so on with the rest.

7

The tents stood at a short distance from the scene of devotion at the well, but not so far as to prevent the spectator from both seeing and hearing what went on in each. Around the well, on bare knees, moved a body of people, thickly wedged together, some praying, some screaming, some excoriating their neighbours' shins, and others dragging them out of their way by the hair of the head. Exclamations of pain from the sick or lame, thumping oaths in Irish, recriminations in broken English, and prayers in bog Latin, all rose at once to the ears of the patron saint, who, we are inclined to think—could he have heard or seen his worshippers—would have disclaimed them altogether.

"For the sake of the Holy Virgin, keep your sharp elbows out o' my ribs."

"My blessin' an you, young man, and don't be lanin' an me, i' you plase!"

"*Damnho sheery orth, a rogarah Ruah!* what do you mane? Is it my back you're breakin'?"

"Hell purshue you, you ould sinner! can't you keep the spike of your crutch out o' my stomach? If you love me tell me so; but, by the livin' farmer, I'll take no such hints as that!"

"I'm a pilgrim, an' don't break my leg upon the rock, an' my blessin' an you!"

"Oh, murdher *sheery!* my poor child 'ill be smodhered!"

"My heart's curse an you! is it the ould cripple you're thrampin' over?"

"Here, Barny, blood alive, give this purty young girl a lift, your sowl, or she'll be undhermost!"

> "'Och, 'twas on a Christmas mornin'
> That Jeeroosillim was born in,
> The Holy Land——'

Oh, my neck's broke!—the curse—Oh! I'm kilt fairly, so I am! The curse o' Cromwell an you, an' hould away——

> 'The Holy Land adornin',
> All by the Baltic Say.
> Three angels on a station,
> All in deep meditation,
> Wor takin' raycrayation,
> All by the——'

Contints o' the book, if you don't hould away, I say agin, an'
let me go an wid my *rann*, it'll be worse for you !—

' Wor takin' raycrayation,
All by the Baltic Say ! ! ' "

" Help the ould woman there."

" Queen o' patriots, pray for us ! St. Abraham—Go to
the divil, you *bosthoon ;* is it crushin' my sore leg you are ?—
St. Abraham pray for us ! St. Isinglass, pray for us ! St.
Jonathan—*Musha*, I wisht you wor in America, honest man,
instid o' twistin' my arm like a gad !—St. Jonathan, pray for
us ! Holy Nineveh, look down upon us wid compression an'
resolution this day ! Blessed Jerooslim, throw down com-
puncture an' meditation upon us Christyeens assembled
here afore you to offer up our sins ! Oh, grant us, blessed
Catasthrophy, the holy virtues of timptation and solitude,
through the improvement an' accommodation of St. Kolumb-
kill ! To him I offer up this button, a bit o' the waistband
o' my own breeches, an' a taste of my wife's petticoat, in
remimbrance of us havin' made this holy station ; an' may
they rise up in glory to prove it for us at the last day !
Amin ! "

Such was the character of the prayers and ejaculations
which issued from the lips of the motley group that
scrambled, and crushed, and screamed on their knees around
the well. In the midst of this ignorance and absurdity there
were visible, however, many instances of apparent piety,
goodness of heart, and simplicity of character. From such
you could hear neither oath nor exclamation. They complied with the usages of the place modestly and attentively ;
though not insensible, at the same time, to the strong disgust
which the general conduct of those who were both superstitious and wicked was calculated to excite. A little from
the well, just where its waters mingled with those of the
cascade, men and women might be seen washing the blood
off their knees, and dipping such parts of their body as were
afflicted with local complaints into the stream. This part of
the ceremony was anything but agreeable to the eye. Most
of those who went round the well drank its waters ; and
several of them filled flasks and bottles with it, which they

brought home for the benefit of such members of their family as could not attend in person.

Whilst all this went forward at the well, scenes of a different kind were enacted lower down among the tents. No sooner had the penitents got the difficult rites of the station over than they were off to the whisky; and decidedly, after the grinding of their bare knees upon the hard rock—after the pushing, crushing, and exhaustion of bodily strength which they had been forced to undergo—we say that the comforts and refreshments to be had in the tents were very seasonable. Here the dancing, shouting, singing, courting, drinking, and fighting formed one wild uproar of noise that was perfectly astounding. The leading boys and the prettiest girls of the parish were all present, partaking in the rustic revelry. Tipsy men were staggering in every direction, fiddles were playing, pipes were squeaking, men were rushing in detached bodies to some fight, women were doctoring the heads of such as had been beaten, and factions were collecting their friends for a fresh battle. Here you might see a grove of shillelahs up, and hear the crash of the onset; and in another place, the heads of the dancing parties bobbing up and down in brisk motion among the crowd that surrounded them. The pilgrim, having now gone through his station, stood hemmed in by a circle of those who wanted to purchase his beads or his scapulars. The ballad-singer had his own mob, from among whom his voice might be heard rising in its purest tones to the praise of

"Brave O'Connell, the Liberathur,
An' great Salvathur of Ireland's Isle!"

As evening approached, the whisky brought out the senseless prejudices of parties and factions in a manner quite consonant to the habits of the people. Those who, in deciding their private quarrels, had in the early part of the day beat and abused each other, now united as the subordinate branches of a greater party for the purpose of opposing in one general body some other hostile faction. These fights are usually commenced by a challenge from one party to another, in which a person from the opposite side is simply

10

and often very good-humouredly invited to assert that "black is the white of his enemy's eye," or to touch the old coat which he is pleased to trail after him between the two opposing powers. This characteristic challenge is soon accepted; the knocking down and yelling are heard; stones fly, and every available weapon is pressed into the service on both sides. In this manner the battle proceeds, until, probably, a life or two is lost. Bones, too, are savagely broken, and blood copiously spilled, by men who scarcely know the remote cause of the enmity between the parties.

Such is a hasty sketch of the Pattern, as it is called in Ireland, at which Larry and Sheelah duly performed their station. We, for our parts, should be sorry to see the innocent pastimes of a people abolished; but surely customs which perpetuate scenes of profligacy and crime should not be suffered to stain the pure and holy character of religion.

It is scarcely necessary to inform our readers that Larry O'Toole and Sheelah complied with every rite of the station. To kiss the "Lucky Stone," however, was their principal duty. Larry gave it a particularly honest smack, and Sheelah impressed it with all the ardour of a devotee. Having refreshed themselves in the tent, they returned home, and in somewhat less than a year from that period found themselves the happy parents of an heir to the half acre, no less a personage than young Phelim, who was called after St. Phelim, the patron of the "Lucky Stone."

The reader perceives that Phelim was born under particularly auspicious influence. His face was the herald of affection everywhere. From the moment of his birth Larry and Sheelah were seldom known to have a dispute. Their whole future life was, with few exceptions, one unchanging honeymoon. Had Phelim been deficient in comeliness, it would have mattered not a *crona bawn*. Phelim, on the contrary, promised to be a beauty; both his parents thought it, felt it, asserted it; and who had a better right to be acquainted, as Larry said, "wid the outs an' ins, the ups an' downs, of his face, the darlin' swaddy?"

For the first ten years of his life Phelim could not be said to owe the tailor much; nor could the covering which he wore be, without more antiquarian lore than we can give to it, exactly classed under any particular term by which the various parts of human dress are known. He himself, like some of our great poets, was externally well acquainted with the elements. The sun and he were particularly intimate; wind and rain were his brothers, and frost also distantly related to him. With mud he was hand and glove, and not a bog in the parish, or a quagmire in the neighbourhood, but sprung up under Phelim's tread, and threw him forward with the brisk vibration of an old acquaintance. Touching his dress, however, in the early part of life, if he was clothed with nothing else, he was clothed with mystery. Some assert that a cast-off pair of his father's nether garments might be seen upon him each Sunday, the wrong side foremost, in accommodation with some economy of his mother's, who thought it safest, in consequence of his habits, to join them in this inverted way to a cape which he wore on his shoulders. We ourselves have seen one who saw another who saw Phelim in a pair of stockings which covered him from his knee-pans to his haunches, where, in the absence of waistbands, they made a pause—a breach existing from that to the small of his back. The person who saw all this affirmed, at the same time, that there was a dearth of cloth about the skirts of the integument which stood him instead of a coat. He bore no bad resemblance, he said, to a moulting fowl, with scanty feathers, running before a gale in the farmyard.

Phelim's want of dress in his merely boyish years being, in a great measure, the national costume of some hundred thousand young Hibernians in his rank of life, deserves a still more particular notice. His infancy we pass over; but from the period at which he did not enter into small-clothes, he might be seen every Sunday morning, or on some important festival, issuing from his father's mansion, with a piece of old cloth tied about him from the middle to the knees, leaving a pair of legs visible that were mottled over with characters which would, if found on an Egyptian pillar, put an antiquary to the necessity of constructing a new alphabet to decipher them. This or the inverted breeches, with his father's flannel waistcoat, or an old coat that swept the ground at least two feet behind him, constituted his state dress. On week days he threw off this finery, and contented himself, if the season

12

were summer, with appearing in a dun-coloured shirt, which resembled a noun-substantive, for it could stand alone. The absence of soap and water is sometimes used as a substitute for milling linen among the lower Irish; and so effectually had Phelim's single change been milled in this manner, that, when disenshirting at night, he usually laid it standing at his bedside, where it reminded one of frosted linen in everything but whiteness.

This, with but little variation, was Phelim's dress until his tenth year. Long before that, however, he evinced those powers of attraction which constituted so remarkable a feature in his character. He won all hearts—the chickens and ducks were devotedly attached to him; the cow, which the family always intended to buy, was in the habit of licking Phelim in his dreams; the two goats, which they actually did buy, treated him like one of themselves. Among the first and last he spent a great deal of his early life; for as the floor of his father's house was but a continuation of the dunghill, or the dunghill a continuation of the floor, we know not rightly which, he had a larger scope and a more unsavoury pool than usual for amusement. Their dunghill, indeed, was the finest of its size and kind to be seen; quite a tasteful thing, and so convenient that he could lay himself down at the hearth and roll out to its foot, after which he ascended it on his legs with all the elasticity of a young poet triumphantly climbing Parnassus.

One of the greatest wants which Phelim experienced in his young days was the want of a capacious pocket. We insinuate nothing; because with respect to his agility in climbing fruit-trees, it was only a species of exercise to which he was addicted—the eating and carrying away of the fruit being merely incidental, or probably the result of abstraction, which, as every one knows, proves what is termed "the absence of genius." In these ambitious exploits, however, there is no denying that he often bitterly regretted the want of a pocket; and in connection with this we have only to add that most of his solitary walks were taken about orchards and gardens, the contents of which he has been seen to contemplate with interest. This, to be sure, might proceed from a provident regard to health, for it is a well-known fact that he has frequently returned home in the evenings distended like a boa constrictor after a gorge ; yet no person was ever able to come at the cause of his inflation. There were, to be sure, suspicions abroad, and it was mostly found that depredations in some neighbouring orchard or garden had been committed a little before the periods in which it was supposed the distension took place. We mention these things, after the example of those "d——d good-natured" biographers who write great men's lives of late, only for the purpose of showing that there could be no truth in such suspicions. Phelim, we assure an enlightened public, was voraciously fond of fruit ; he was frequently inflated, too, after the manner of those who indulge therein to excess—fruit was always missed immediately after the periods of his distension, so that it was impossible he could have been concerned in the depredations then made upon the neighbouring orchards. In addition to this we would beg modestly to add that the pomonian temperament is incompatible with the other qualities for which he was famous. His parents were too ignorant of those little eccentricities, which, had they known them, would have opened up a correct view of the splendid materials for village greatness which he possessed, and which probably were nipped in their bud for the want of a pocket to his breeches, or rather by the want of breeches to his pocket, for such was the wayward energy of his disposition that he ultimately succeeded in getting the latter, though it certainly often failed him to procure the breeches. In fact, it was a misfortune to him that he was the son of his father and mother at all. Had he been a second Melchizedec, and got into breeches in time, the virtues which circumstances suppressed in his heart might have flourished like cauliflowers, though the world would have lost all the advantages arising from the splendour of his talents at going naked.

Another fact, in justice to his character, must not be omitted. His penchant for fruit was generally known ; but few persons, at the period we are describing, were at all aware that a love of whisky lurked as a predominant trait in his character, to be brought out at a future era in his life.

Before Phelim reached his tenth year he and his parents had commenced hostilities. Many were their efforts to subdue

14

some peculiarities of his temper which then began to appear. Phelim, however, being an only son, possessed high vantage-ground. Along with other small matters which he was in the habit of picking up, might be reckoned a readiness at swearing. Several other things also made their appearance in his parents' cottage, for whose presence there, except through his instrumentality, they found it rather difficult to account. Spades, shovels, rakes, tubs, frying-pans, and many other articles of domestic use were transferred, as if by magic, to Larry's cabin.

As Larry and his wife were both honest, these things were of course restored to their owners the moment they could be ascertained. Still, although this honest couple's integrity was known, there were many significant looks turned upon Phelim, and many spirited prophecies uttered with especial reference to him, all of which hinted at the probability of his dying something in the shape of a perpendicular death. This habit, then, of adding to their furniture was one cause of the hostility between him and his parents—we say one, for there were at least a good round dozen besides. His touch, for instance, was fatal to crockery; he stripped his father's Sunday clothes of their buttons with great secrecy and skill; he was a dead shot at the panes of his neighbours' windows; a perfect necromancer at sucking eggs through pin-holes; took great delight in calling home the neighbouring farmers' work-men to dinner an hour before it was ready; and was, in fact, a perfect master in many other ingenious manifestations of character ere he reached his twelfth year.

Now it was about this period that the smallpox made its appearance in the village. Indescribable was the dismay of Phelim's parents lest he among others might become a victim to it. Vaccination had not then surmounted the prejudices with which every discovery beneficial to mankind is at first met; and the people were left principally to the imposture of quacks, or the cunning of certain persons called "fairy men" or "sonsie" women. Nothing remained now but that this formidable disease should be met by all the power and resources of superstition. The first thing the mother did was to get a gospel consecrated by the priest, for the purpose of guarding Phelim against evil. What is termed a gospel, and

15

worn as a kind of charm about the person, is simply a slip of paper on which are written by the priest the first few verses of the Gospel of St. John. This, however, being worn for no specific purpose, was incapable of satisfying the honest woman. Superstition had its own peculiar remedy for the smallpox, and Sheelah was resolved to apply it. Accordingly she borrowed a neighbour's ass, drove it home, with Phelim, however, on its back, took the interesting youth by the nape of the neck, and in the name of the Trinity shoved him three times under it and three times over it. She then put a bit of bread into its mouth, until the ass had mumbled it a little, after which she gave the savoury morsel to Phelim as a *bonne bouche*. This was one preventive against the smallpox; but another was to be tried.

She next clipped off the extremities of Phelim's elf-locks, tied them in linen that was never bleached, and hung them beside the gospel about his neck. This was her second cure; but there was still a third to be applied. She got the largest onion possible, which, having cut it into nine parts, she hung from the roof-tree of the cabin, having first put the separated parts together. It is supposed that this has the power of drawing infection of any kind to itself. It is permitted to remain untouched until the disease has passed from the neighbourhood, when it is buried as far down in the earth as a single man can dig. This was a third cure; but there was still a fourth. She borrowed ten asses' halters from her neighbours, who, on hearing that they were for Phelim's use, felt particular pleasure in obliging her. Having procured these, she pointed them one by one at Phelim's neck, until the number nine was completed. The tenth she put on him, and with the end of it in her hand, led him like an ass, nine mornings before sunrise, to a south-running stream, which he was obliged to cross. On doing this, two conditions were to be fulfilled on the part of Phelim: he was bound, in the first place, to keep his mouth filled, during the ceremony, with a certain fluid which must be nameless; in the next, to be silent from the moment he left home until his return.

Sheelah, having satisfied herself that everything calculated to save her darling from the smallpox was done, felt considerably relieved, and hoped that, whoever might be

infected, Phelim would escape. On the morning when the
last journey to the river had been completed, she despatched
him home with the halters. Phelim, however, wended his
way to a little hazel copse below the house, where he deliberately twined the halters together, and erected a swing-
swang, with which he amused himself till hunger brought
him to his dinner.

"Phelim, you 'idle thief, what kep' you away till now ? "

"Oh, mudher, mudher, gi' me a piece o' *arran*" (bread).

"Why, here's the praties done for your dinner. What
kep' you ? "

"Oh, begorra, it's well you ever see me at all, so it is ? "

"Why," said his father, "what happened you ? "

"Oh, bedad, a terrible thing all out. As I was crassin'
Dunroe Hill, I thramped on hungry grass.[1] First I didn't
know what kem over me, I got so wake; and every step I
wint 'twas waker an' waker I was growin', till at long last
down I dhrops, and couldn't move hand or fut. I dunna
how long I lay there, so I don't; but, anyhow, who should
be *sthreelin'* acrass the hill but an ould *boccagh*.

"'My *bouchaleen dhas*,' says he, 'you're in a bad state I
find. You've thramped upon Dunroe hungry grass, an' only
for somethin' it's a *prabeen* you'd be afore ever you'd see
home. Can you spake at all ? ' says he.

"'Oh, murdher,' says I, 'I b'lieve not.'

"'Well, here,' says the *boccagh*, 'open your purty *gob*, an'
take in a thrifle of this male, an' you'll soon be stout enough.'
Well, to be sure, it bates the world ! I had hardly tasted
the male, whin I found myself as well as ever; bekase, you
know, mudher, that's the cure for it. 'Now,' says the
boccagh, 'this is the spot the fairies planted their hungry
grass an, so you'll know it agin when you see it. What's
your name ? ' says he.

"'Phelim O'Toole,' says I.

"'Well,' says he, 'go home an' tell your father an' mother
to offer up a prayer to St. Phelim, your namesake, in regard

---

[1] This refers to a superstition (which Carleton has illustrated in
another story) of the people, who believe that grass which fairies have
chosen affects the mortals who walk on it with a feeling of excessive
hunger.

that only for him you'd be a *corp* before any relief would a come near you—or, at any rate, wid the fairies.'"

The father and mother, although with a thousand proofs before them that Phelim, so long as he could at all contrive a lie, would never speak truth, yet were so blind to his well-known propensity that they always believed the lie to be truth until they discovered it to be a falsehood. When he related a story, for instance, which carried not only improbability, but impossibility, on the face of it, they never questioned his veracity. The neighbours, to be sure, were vexed and nettled at the obstinacy of their credulity, especially on reflecting that they were as sceptical in giving credence to the narrative of any other person as all rational people ought to be. The manner of training up Phelim, and Phelim's method of governing them, had become a by-word in the village. "Take a sthraw to him, like Sheelah O'Toole," was often ironically said to mothers remarkable for mischievous indulgence to their children.

The following day proved that no charm could protect Phelim from the smallpox. Every symptom of that disease became quite evident; and the grief of his doting parents amounted to distraction. Neither of them could be declared perfectly sane; they knew not how to proceed—what regimen to adopt for him, nor what remedies to use. A week elapsed, but each succeeding day found him in a more dangerous state. At length, by the advice of some of the neighbours, an old crone called "Sonsie Mary" was called in to administer relief through the medium of certain powers which were thought to be derived from something holy and also supernatural. She brought a mysterious bottle, of which he was to take every third spoonful three times a day; it was to be administered by the hand of a young girl of virgin innocence, who was also to breathe three times down his throat, holding his nostrils closed with her fingers. The father and mother were to repeat a certain number of prayers, to promise against swearing, and to kiss the hearthstone nine times—the one turned north, and the other south. All these ceremonies were performed with care, but Phelim's malady appeared to set them at defiance; and the old crone would have lost her character in consequence, were it not that

18

Larry, on the day of the cure, after having promised not to swear, let fly an oath at a hen whose cackling disturbed Phelim. This saved her character, and threw Larry and Sheelah into fresh despair.

They had nothing now for it but the "fairy man," to whom, despite the awful mystery of his character, they resolved to apply rather than see their only son taken from them for ever. Larry proceeded without delay to the wise man's residence, after putting a small phial of holy water in his pocket to protect himself from fairy influence. The house in which this person lived was admirably in accordance with his mysterious character. One gable of it was formed by the mound of a fairy *rath*, against which the cabin stood endwise. Within a mile there was no other building; the country around it was a sheep-walk, green, and beautifully interspersed with two or three solitary glens, in one of which might be seen a cave, that was said to communicate under ground with the *rath*. A ridge of high-peaked mountains ran above it, whose evening shadow, in consequence of their form, fell down on each side of the *rath*, without obscuring its precincts. It lay south; and such was the power of superstition, that during summer the district in which it stood was thought to be covered with a light and silence decidedly supernatural. In spring it was the first to be in verdure, and in autumn the last. Nay, in winter itself the *rath* and the adjoining valleys never ceased to be green. These circumstances were not attributed to the nature of the soil, to its southern situation, nor to the fact of its being pasture-land, but simply to the power of the fairies, who were supposed to keep its verdure fresh for their own revels.

When Larry entered the house, which had an air of comfort and snugness beyond the common, a tall thin pike of a man, about sixty years of age, stood before him. He wore a brown greatcoat that fell far short of his knees; his small-clothes were closely fitted to thighs not thicker than hand telescopes; on his legs were drawn grey woollen stockings, rolled up about six inches over his small-clothes; his head was covered by a bay bobwig, on which was a little round hat, with the edge of the leaf turned up in every direction. His face was short and sallow, his chin peaked, his nose small and turned up. If we add to this a pair of skeleton-like hands and arms projecting about eight inches beyond the sleeves of his coat, two fiery-ferret eyes, and a long, small hollow wand higher than himself, we have the outline of this singular figure.

"God save you, nabour," said Larry.

"Save you, save you, nabour," he replied, without pronouncing the name of the deity.

"This is a thryin' time," said Larry, "to them that has childher."

The fairy man fastened his red glittering eyes upon him with a sinister glance that occasioned Larry to feel rather uncomfortable.

"So you venthured to come to the fairy man?"

"It is about our son, an' he all we ha——"

"Whisht!" said the man, waving his hand with a commanding air. "Whisht! I wish you wor out o' this, for it's a bad time to be here. Listen! Listen! Do you hear nothing?"

Larry changed colour. "I do," he replied—"the Lord protect me! Is that them?".[1]

"What did you hear?" said the man.

"Why," returned the other, "I heard the bushes of the *rath* all movin', just as if a blast o' wind came among them!"

"Whisht!" said the fairy man, "they're here; you mustn't open your lips while you're in the house. I know what you want, an' we'll see your son. Do you hear anything more? If you do, lay your forefinger along your nose; but don't spake."

Larry heard, with astonishment, the music of a pair of bagpipes. The tune played was one which, according to a popular legend, was first played by Satan; it is called "Go to the Devil and Shake Yourself." To our own knowledge the peasantry in certain parts of Ireland refuse to sing it for the above reason. The mystery of the music was heightened, too, by the fact of its being played, as Larry thought, behind the gable of the cabin which stood against the side of the *rath*, out of which, indeed, it seemed to proceed.

---

[1] The fairies.

Larry laid his finger along his nose, as he had been desired; and this appearing to satisfy the fairy man, he waved his hand to the door, thus intimating that his visitor should depart; which he did immediately, but not without observing that this wild-looking being closed and bolted the door after him.

It is unnecessary to say that he was rather anxious to get off the premises of the good people; he therefore lost little time until he arrived at his own cabin; but judge of his wonder when, on entering it, he found the long-legged spectre awaiting his return.

"*Bonaght dhea orrin!*" he exclaimed, starting back; "the blessin' o' God be upon us! Is it here before me you are?"

"Hould your tongue, man," said the other, with a smile of mysterious triumph. "Is it that you wondher at? Ha, ha! That's little of it!"

"But how did you know my name? or who I was? or where I lived at all? Heaven protect us! it's beyant belief, clane out."

"Hould your tongue," replied the man; "don't be axin' me anything o' the kind. Clear out, both of yees, till I begin my *pisthrogues* wid the sick child. Clear out, I say."

With some degree of apprehension Larry and Sheelah left the house as they had been ordered, and the fairy man, having pulled out a flask of *poteen*, administered a dose of it to Phelim; and never yet did patient receive his medicine with such a relish: he licked his lips, and fixed his eye upon it with a longing look.

"Begorra," said he, "that's fine stuff entirely. Will you lave me the bottle?"

"No," said the fairy man; "but I'll call an' give you a little of it wanst a day."

"Ay, do," replied Phelim; "the divil a fear o' me if I get enough of it. I hope I'll see you often."

The fairy man kept his word; so that what with his bottle, a hardy constitution, and light bedclothes, Phelim got the upper hand of his malady. In a month he was again on his legs; but, alas! his complexion, though not changed to deformity, was woefully out of joint. His principal blemish, in addition to the usual marks left by this complaint, consisted in a drooping of his left eyelid, which gave to his whole face a cast highly ludicrous.

When Phelim felt thoroughly recovered, he claimed a pair of "leather crackers," a hareskin cap, and a coat, with a pertinacity which kept the worthy couple in a state of inquietude until they complied with his importunity. Henceforth he began to have everything his own way. His parents, sufficiently thankful that he was spared to them, resolved to thwart him no more.

"It's well we have him at all," said his mother; "sure, if we hadn't him, we'd be breakin' our hearts, and sayin', if it ud plase God to send him back to us, that we'd be happy even wid givin' him his own way."

"They say it breaks their strinth, too," replied his father, "to be crubbin' them in too much, an' snappin' at thim for every hand's turn; an' I'm sure it does too."

"Doesn't he become the pock-marks well, the crathur?" said the mother.

"Become!" said the father—"but doesn't the droop in his eye set him off all to pieces!"

"Ay," observed the mother; "an' how the crathur went round among all the neighbours to show them the 'leather crackers'! To see his little pride out o' the hareskin cap, too, wid the hare's ears stickin' out of his temples—that, an' the droopin' eye undher them, makes him look so cunnin' an' ginteel that one can't help havin' their heart fixed upon him."

"He'd look betther still if that ould coat wasn't sweepin' the ground behind him; an' what ud you think to put a pair o' *martyeens* on his legs to hide the mazles? He might go anywhere thin."

"Throth, he might. But, Larry, what in the world wide could be in the fairy man's bottle that Phelim took sich a likin' for it? He tould me this mornin' that he'd suffer to have the pock agin, set in case he was cured wid the same bottle."

"Well, the heaven be praised, anyhow, that we have a son for the half acre, Sheelah."

"Amin! An' let us take good care of him, now that he's spared to us."

22

Phelim's appetite after his recovery was anything but a joke to his father. He was now seldom at home, except during meal-times; wherever fun or novelty was to be found, Phelim was present. He became a regular attendant upon all the sportsmen. To such he made himself very useful by his correct knowledge of the best covers for game and the best pools for fish. He was acquainted with every rood of land in the parish; knew with astonishing accuracy where coveys were to be sprung and hares started. No hunt was without him; such was his wind and speed of foot that to follow a chase, and keep up with the horsemen, was to him only a matter of sport. When daylight passed, night presented him with amusements suitable to itself. No wake, for instance, could escape him; a dance without young Phelim O'Toole would have been a thing worthy to be remembered. He was zealously devoted to cock-fighting; on Shrove-Tuesday he shouted loudest among the crowd that attended the sport of throwing at cocks tied to a stake; football and hurling never occurred without him; bull-baiting, for it was common in his youth, was luxury to him; and ere he reached fourteen every one knew Phelim O'Toole as an adept at card-playing. Wherever a sheep, a leg of mutton, a dozen of bread, or a bottle of whisky was put up in a shebeen-house, to be played for by the country gamblers at the five and ten, or spoiled five, Phelim always took a hand, and was generally successful. On these occasions he was frequently charged with an over-refined dexterity; but Phelim usually swore, in vindication of his own innocence, until he got black in the face, as the phrase among such characters goes.

The reader is to consider him now about fifteen, a stout, overgrown, unwashed cub. His parents' anxiety that he should grow strong prevented them from training him to any kind of employment. He was eternally going about in quest of diversion; and wherever a knot of idlers was to be found, there was Phelim. He had, up to this period, never wore a shoe, nor a single article of dress that had been made for himself, with the exception of one or two pair of sheepskin small-clothes. In this way he passed his time, bare-legged, without shoes, clothed in an old coat much too large for him, his neck open, and his sooty locks covered with the hareskin

23

cap, the ears, as usual, sticking out above his brows. Much of his time was spent in setting the idle boys of the village to fight, and in carrying lying challenges from one to another. He himself was seldom without a broken head or a black eye; for, in Ireland, he who is known to be fond of quarrelling, as the people say, usually "gets enough an' lavins of it." Larry and Sheelah, thinking it now high time that something should be done with Phelim, thought it necessary to give him some share of education. Phelim opposed this bitterly as an unjustifiable encroachment upon his personal liberty; but by bribing him with the first and only suit of clothes he had yet got, they at length succeeded in prevailing on him to go.

The school to which he was sent happened to be kept in what is called an Inside Kiln. This kind of kiln is usually —but less so now than formerly—annexed to respectable farmers' outhouses, to which, in agricultural districts, it forms a very necessary appendage. It also serves at the same time as a barn, the kiln-pot being sunk in the shape of an inverted cone at one end, but divided from the barn-floor by a wall about three feet high. From this wall beams run across the kiln-pot, over which, in a transverse direction, are laid a number of rafters like the joists of a loft, but not fastened. These ribs are covered with straw, over which again is spread a winnow cloth to keep the grain from being lost. The fire is sunk on a level with the bottom of the kiln-pot—that is, about eight or ten feet below the floor of the barn. The descent to it is by stairs formed at the side wall. We have been thus minute in describing it because, as the reader will presently perceive, the feats of Phelim render it necessary.

On the first day of his entering the school he presented himself with a black eye; and as his character was well known to both master and scholars, the former felt no hesitation in giving him a wholesome lecture upon the subject of his future conduct. For at least a year before this time he had gained the nickname of "Blessed Phelim," and "Bouncing," epithets bestowed on him by an ironical allusion to his patron saint and his own habits.

"So, Blessed Phelim," said the master, "you are coming to school!! Well, well! I only say that miracles will never cease. *Arrah*, Phelim, will you tell us candidly—ah—I beg

24

your pardon—I mean, will you tell us the best lie you can coin upon the cause of your coming to imbibe moral and literary knowledge? Silence, boys, till we hear Blessed Phelim's lie."

"You must hear it, masther," said Phelim. "I'm comin' to larn to read an' write."

"Bravo! By the bones of Prosodius, I expected a lie, but not such a thumper as that. And you're comin' wid a black eye to prove it! A black eye, Phelim, is the blackguard's coat-of-arms; and to do you justice, you are seldom widout your crest."

For a few days Phelim attended the school, but learned not a letter. The master usually sent him to be taught by the youngest lads, with a hope of being able to excite a proper spirit of pride and emulation in a mind that required some extraordinary impulse. One day he called him up to ascertain what progress he had actually made; the unsuspecting teacher sat at the time upon the wall which separated the barn-floor from the kiln-pot, with his legs dangling at some distance from the ground. It was summer, and the rafters used in drying the grain had been removed. On finding that Blessed Phelim, notwithstanding all the lessons he had received, was still in a state of the purest ignorance, he lost his temper, and brought him over between his knees, that he might give him an occasional cuff for his idleness. The lesson went on, and the master's thumps were thickening about Phelim's ears, much to the worthy youth's displeasure.

" Phelim," said the master, " I'll invert you as a scarecrow for dunces. I'll lay you against the wall, with your head down and your heels up, like a forked carrot."

" But how will you manage that? " said Phelim. " What ud I be doin' in the manetime ? "

" I'll find a way to manage it," said the master.

" To put my head down an' my heels up, is id? " inquired Phelim.

" You've said it, my worthy," returned his teacher.

" If you don't know the way," replied the pupil, " I'll show you," getting his shoulder under the master's leg, and pitching him heels over head into the kiln-pot. He instantly seized his cap, and ran out of the school, highly delighted at his feat, leaving the scholars to render the master whatever assistance was necessary. The poor man was not dangerously hurt; but in addition to a broken arm, he received half a dozen severe contusions on the head and in different parts of the body.

This closed Phelim's education; for no persuasion could ever induce him to enter a school afterwards; nor could any temptation prevail on the neighbouring teachers to admit him as a pupil.

Phelim now shot up rapidly to the stature of a young man; and a graceful slip was he. From the period of fifteen until nineteen he was industriously employed in idleness. About sixteen he began to look after the girls, and to carry a cudgel. The father in vain attempted to inoculate him with a love of labour; but Phelim would not receive the infection. His life was a pleasanter one. Sometimes, indeed, when he wanted money to treat the girls at fairs and markets, he would prevail on himself to labour a week or fortnight with some neighbouring farmer; but the moment he had earned as much as he deemed sufficient, the spade was thrown aside. Phelim knew all the fiddlers and pipers in the barony; was master of the ceremonies at every wake and dance that occurred within several miles of him. He was a crack dancer, and never attended a dance without performing a hornpipe on a door or a table. No man could shuffle, or treble, or cut, or spring, or caper with him. Indeed, it was said that he could dance "Moll Roe" upon the end of a five-gallon keg, and snuff a mould candle with his heels, yet never lose the time. The father and mother were exceedingly proud of Phelim. The former, when he found him grown up, and associating with young men, began to feel a kind of ambition in being permitted to join Phelim and his companions, and to look upon the society of his own son as a privilege. With the girls Phelim was a beauty without paint. They thought every wake truly a scene of sorrow if he did not happen to be present. Every dance was doleful without him. Phelim wore his hat on one side, with a knowing but careless air; he carried his cudgel with a good-humoured dashing spirit, precisely in accordance with the character of a man who did not care a *traneen* whether he drank with you

26

as a friend, or fought with you as a foe. Never were such songs heard as Phelim could sing, nor such a voice as that with which he sang them. His attitudes and action were inimitable. The droop in his eye was a standing wink at the girls ; and when he sang his funny songs, with what practised ease he gave the darlings a roguish chuck under the chin ! Then his jokes ! "Why, faix," as the fair ones often said of him, "before Phelim speaks at all, one laughs at what he says." This was fact. His very appearance at a wake, dance, or drinking match was hailed by a peal of mirth. This heightened his humour exceedingly ; for say what you will, laughter is to wit what air is to fire—the one dies without the other.

Let no one talk of beauty being on the surface. This is a popular error, and no one but a superficial fellow would defend it. Among ten thousand you could not get a more unfavourable surface than Phelim's. His face resembled the rough side of a colander,[1] or, as he was often told in raillery, "you might grate potatoes on it." The lid of his right eye, as the reader knows, was like the lid of a salt-box, always closed ; and when he risked a wink with the left, it certainly gave him the look of a man shutting out the world and retiring into himself for the purpose of self-examination. No, no ; beauty is in the mind, in the soul ; otherwise Phelim never could have been such a prodigy of comeliness among the girls. This was the distinction the fair sex drew in his favour. "Phelim," they would say, "is not purty, but he's very comely." "Bad end to the one of him but would stale a pig off a tether wid his winnin' ways." And so he would too, without much hesitation, for it was not the first time he had stolen his father's.

From nineteen until the close of his minority, Phelim became a distinguished man in fairs and markets. He was, in fact, the hero of the parish ; but unfortunately he seldom knew on the morning of the fair-day the name of the party or faction on whose side he was to fight. This was merely a matter of priority, for whoever happened to give him the first treat uniformly secured him. The reason of this pliability

---

[1] Sometimes called cullender.

on his part was that Phelim, being every person's friend by his good-nature, was nobody's foe except for the day. He fought for fun and whisky. When he happened to drub some companion or acquaintance on the opposite side, he was ever ready to express his regret at the circumstance, and abused them heartily for not having treated him first.

Phelim was also a great Ribbonman; and from the time he became initiated into the system, his eyes were wonderfully opened to the oppressions of the country. Sessions, decrees, and warrants he looked upon as gross abuses; assizes, too, by which so many of his friends were put to some inconvenience, he considered as the result of Protestant ascendency —cancers that ought to be cut out of the constitution. Bailiffs, drivers, tithe-proctors, tax-gatherers, policemen, and parsons he thought were vermin that ought to be compelled to emigrate to a much warmer country than Ireland.

There was no such hand in the country as Phelim at an *alibi*. Just give him the outline—a few leading particulars of the fact—and he would work wonders. One would think, indeed, that he had been born for that especial purpose; for as he was never known to utter a syllable of truth but once, when he had a design in not being believed, so there was no risk of a lawyer getting truth out of him. No man was ever afflicted with such convenient maladies as Phelim; even his sprains, toothaches, and colics seemed to have entered into the Whiteboy system. But, indeed, the very diseases in Ireland are seditious. Many a time has a toothachè come in to aid Paddy in obstructing the course of justice, and a colic been guilty of misprision of treason. Irish deaths, too, are very disloyal, and frequently at variance with the laws. Nor are our births much better; for although more legitimate than those of our English neighbours, yet they are in general more illegal. Phelim, in proving his *alibis*, proved all these positions. On one occasion "he slep' at the prisoner's house, and couldn't close his eye with a thief of a toothache that parsecuted him the whole night;" so that, in consequence of having the toothache, it was impossible that the prisoner could leave the house without his knowledge.

Again, the prisoner at the bar could not possibly have shot the deceased, "bekase Mickey slep' that very night at

Phelim's, an' Phelim, bein' ill o' the colic, never slep' at all durin' the whole night; an', by the vartue of his oath, the poor boy couldn't go out o' the house unknownst to him. If he had, Phelim would a seen him, sure."

Again, "Paddy Cummisky's wife tuck ill of a young one, an' Phelim was sent for to bring the midwife; but afore he kem to Paddy's or hard o' the thing at all, the prisoner, arly in the night, comin' to sit a while wid Paddy, went for the midwife instead o' Phelim, an' thin they sot up an' had a sup in regard of the 'casion, an' the prisoner never left them at all that night until the next mornin'. An' by the same a-token, he remimbered Paddy Cummisky barrin' the door, an' shuttin' the windies, bekase it's not lucky to have them open, for 'fraid that the fairies ud throw their *pishthrogues* upon the young one, an' it not christened."

Phelim was certainly an accomplished youth. As an alibist, however, his career was, like that of all alibists, a short one. The fact was, that his face soon became familiar to the court and the lawyers, so that his name and appearance were ultimately rather hazardous to the cause of his friends.

Phelim, on other occasions, when summoned as evidence against his well-wishers or brother Ribbonmen, usually forgot his English, and gave his testimony by an interpreter. Nothing could equal his ignorance and want of common capacity during these trials. His face was as free from every visible trace of meaning as if he had been born an idiot. No block was ever more impenetrable than he.

"What is the noble gintleman sayin'?" he would ask in Irish; and on having that explained, he would inquire, "What is that?" then demand a fresh explanation of the last one, and so on successively, until he was given up in despair.

Sometimes, in cases of a capital nature, Phelim, with the consent of his friends, would come forward and make disclosures, in order to have them put upon their trial and acquitted, lest an approver, or some one earnestly disposed to prosecute, might appear against them. Now the *alibi* and its usual accompaniments are all of old standing in Ireland; but the master-stroke to which we have alluded is a modern invention. Phelim would bear evidence against them; and

29

whilst the Government—for it was mostly in Government prosecutions he adventured this—believed they had ample grounds for conviction in his disclosures, it little suspected that the whole matter was a plan to defeat itself. In accordance with his design, he gave such evidence upon the table as rendered conviction hopeless. His great object was to damn his own character as a witness, and to make such blunders, premeditated slips, and admissions, as just left him within an inch of a prosecution for perjury. Having succeeded in acquitting his friends, he was content to withdraw amid a volley of pretended execrations, leaving the attorney-general, with all his legal knowledge, outwitted and foiled.

All Phelim's accomplishments, however, were nothing when compared to his gallantry. With personal disadvantages which would condemn any other man to old bachelorship, he was nevertheless the white-headed boy among the girls. He himself was conscious of this, and made his attacks upon their hearts indiscriminately. If he met an unmarried female only for five minutes, be she old or ugly, young or handsome, he devoted at least four minutes and three-quarters to the tender passion—made love to her with an earnestness that would deceive a saint, backed all his protestations with a superfluity of round oaths, and drew such a picture of her beauty as might suit the houries of Mahomet's paradise.

Phelim and his father were great associates. No two agreed better. They went to fairs and markets together, got drunk together, and returned home with their arms about each other's neck in the most loving and affectionate manner. Larry, if Phelim were too modest to speak for himself, seldom met a young girl without laying siege to her for the son. He descanted upon his good qualities, glossed over his defects, and drew deeply upon invention in his behalf. Sheelah, on the other hand, was an eloquent advocate for him. She had her eye upon half a dozen of the village girls, to every one of whom she found something to say in Phelim's favour.

But it is time the action of our story should commence. When Phelim had reached his twenty-fifth year the father thought it was high time for him to marry. The good man had, of course, his own motives for this. In the first place, Phelim, with all his gallantry and cleverness, had never contributed a shilling either towards his own support or that of the family. In the second place, he was never likely to do so. In the third place, the father found him a bad companion; for, in good truth, he had corrupted the good man's morals so evidently that his character was now little better than that of his son. In the fourth place, he never thought of Phelim that he did not see a gallows in the distance; and matrimony, he thought, might save him from hanging, as one poison neutralises another. In the fifth place, the half acre was but a shabby patch to meet the exigencies of the family since Phelim grew up. "Bouncing Phelim," as he was called for more reasons than one, had the gift of good digestion along with his other accomplishments, and with such energy was it exercised that the "half acre" was frequently in hazard of leaving the family altogether. The father therefore felt quite willing, if Phelim married, to leave him the inheritance, and seek a new settlement for himself. Or if Phelim preferred leaving him, he agreed to give him one-half of it, together with an equal division of all his earthly goods: to wit—two goats, of which Phelim was to get one; six hens and a cock, of which Phelim was to get three hens and the chance of a toss-up for the cock; four stools, of which Phelim was to get two; two pots—a large one and a small one—the former to go with Phelim; three horn spoons, of which Phelim was to get one and the chance of a toss-up for the third. Phelim was to bring his own bed, provided he did not prefer getting a bottle of fresh straw as a connubial luxury. The blanket was a tender subject; for having been fourteen years in employment, it entangled the father and Phelim touching the prudence of the latter claiming it all. The son was at length compelled to give it up, at least in the character of an appendage to his marriage property. He feared that the wife, should he not be able to replace it by a new one, or should she herself not be able to bring him one as part of her dowry, would find the honeymoon rather lively. Phelim's bedstead admitted of no dispute, the floor of the cabin having served him in that capacity ever since he began to sleep in a separate bed. His pillow was his small-clothes, and his quilt his own coat, under which he slept snugly enough.

The father having proposed, and the son acceded to, these arrangements, the next thing to be done was to pitch upon a proper girl as his wife. This, being a more important matter, was thus discussed by the father and son one evening at their own fireside, in the presence of Sheelah.

"Now, Phelim," said the father, "look about you, an' tell us what girl in the neighbourhood you'd like to be married to."

"Why," replied Phelim, "I'll lave that to you; jist point out the girl you'd like for your daughther-in-law, an' be she rich, poor, ould, or ugly, I'll delude her. That's the chat."

"Ah, Phelim, if you could put your *comedher* an Gracey Dalton, you'd be a made boy. She has the full of a rabbit-skin o' guineas."

"A made boy! Faith, they say I'm that as it is, you know. But would you wish me to put my *comedher* on Gracey Dalton? Spake out."

"To be sure I would."

"Ay," observed the mother; "or what ud you think of Miss Pattherson? That ud be the girl. She has a fine farm and five hundher pounds. She's a Protestant, but Phelim could make a Christian of her."

"To be sure I could," said Phelim, "have her thumpin' her breast and countin' her *Padareens* in no time. Would you wish me to have her, mudher?"

"Throth an' I would, *avick*."

"That ud never do," observed the father. "Sure, you don't think she'd ever think of the likes o' Phelim?"

"Don't make a goose of yourself, ould man," observed Phelim. "Do you think, if I set about it, that I'd not manufacture her senses as asy as I'd peel a piatee."

"Well, well," replied the father, "in the name o' goodness make up to her. Faith, it ud be something to have a jauntin'-car in the family."

"Ay, but what the sorra will I do for a suit o' clothes," observed Phelim. "I could never go near her in these breeches. My elbows, too, are out o' this ould coat, bad luck to it! An' as for a waistcoat, why, I dunna but it's a sin to call what I'm wearin' a waistcoat at all. Thin agin— why, blood alive, sure I can't go to her barefooted; an' I dunna but it ud be dacenter to do that same than to step out in sich excuses for brogues as these. An' in regard o' the stockins, why, I've pulled them down, sthrivin' to look dacent, till one ud think the balls o' my legs is at my heels."

"The sorra word's in that but thruth, anyhow," observed the father; "but what's to be done?—for we have no way of gettin' them."

"Faith, I don't know that," said Phelim. "What if we'd borry? I could get the loan of a pair of breeches from Dudley Dwire, an' a coat from Sam Appleton. We might thry Billy Brady for a waistcoat an' a pair o' stockins. Barny Buckram-back, the pinsioner, ud lend me his pumps; an' we want nothing now but a hat."

"Nothin' undher a Caroline ud do, goin' there," observed the father.

"I think Father Carroll ud oblage me wid the loan o' one for a day or two," said Phelim; "he has two or three o' them, all as good as ever."

"But, Phelim," said the father, "before we go to all this trouble, are you sure you could put your *comedher* on Miss Pattherson?"

"None o' your nonsense," said Phelim; "don't you know I could? I hate a man to be puttin' questions to me when he knows them himself. It's a fashion you have got, an' you ought to dhrop it."

"Well, thin," said the father, "let us set about it to-morrow. If we can borry the clo'es, thry your luck."

Phelim and the father, the next morning, set out, each in a different direction, to see how far they could succeed on the borrowing system. The father was to make a descent on Dudley Dwire for the breeches, and appeal to the generosity of Sam Appleton for the coat. Phelim himself was to lay his case before the priest, and to assail Buckram-back, the pensioner, on his way home for the brogues.

When Phelim arrived at the priest's house, he found none of the family up but the housekeeper. After bidding her good-morrow, and being desired to sit down, he entered into conversation with the good woman, who felt anxious to know the scandal of the whole parish.

"Aren't you a son of Larry Toole's, young man?"

"I am, indeed, Mrs. Doran. I'm Phelim O'Toole, my mother says."

"I hope you're comin' to spake to the priest about your duty?"

"Why, then, begorra, I'm glad you axed me, so I am—for only you seen the pinance in my face, you'd never suppose sich a thing. I want to make my confishion to him, wid the help o' goodness."

"Is there any news goin', Phelim?"

"Divil a much, barrin' what you hard yourself, I suppose, about Frank Fogarty, that went mad yestherday, for risin' the meal on the poor, an' ate the ears off himself afore anybody could see him."

"*Vick na hoia*, Phelim; do you tell me so?"

"Why, man o' Moses! is it possible you did not hear it, ma'am?"

"Oh, *wurrah*, man alive, not a syllable! Ate the ears off of himself! Phelim, *acushla*, see what it is to be hard an the poor!"

"Oh, he was ever an' always the biggest nager livin', ma'am. Ay, an' when he was tied up till a blessed priest ud be brought to *malivogue* the divil out of him, he got a scythe an' cut his own two hands off."

"No, thin, Phelim."

"Faitha, ma'am, sure enough. I suppose, ma'am, you hard about Biddy Duignan?"

"Who is she, Phelim?"

"Why, the misfortunate crathur's a daughter of her father's, ould Mick Duignan, of Tavenimore."

"An' what about her, Phelim? What happened her?"

"Faix, ma'am, a bit of a mistake she met wid; but, anyhow, ould Harry Connolly's to stand in the chapel nine Sundays, an' to make three stations to Lough Derg for it. Bedad, they say it's as purty a crathur as you'd see in a day's thravellin'."

"Harry Connolly! Why, I know Harry, but I never heard of Biddy Duignan or her father at all. Harry Connolly! Is it a man that's bent over his staff for the last twenty years? Hut, tut, Phelim, don't say sich a thing!"

"Why, ma'am, sure he takes wid it himself; he doesn't deny it at all, the ould sinner."

"Oh, that I mayn't sin, Phelim, if one knows who to thrust in this world, so they don't. Why, the desateful ould—Hut, Phelim, I can't give in to it."

"Faix, ma'am, no wondher; but sure, when he confesses it himself! Bedad, Mrs. Doran, I never seen you look so well. Upon my sowl, you'd take the shine out o' the youngest o' thim!"

"Is it me, Phelim? Why, you're beside yourself."

"Beside myself, am I? Faith, an' if I am, what I said's thruth, anyhow. I'd give more nor I'll name to have so red a pair of cheeks as you have. Sowl, they're thumpers."

"Ha, ha, ha! Oh, that I mayn't sin, but that's a good joke! An ould woman, near sixty!"

"Now, Mrs. Doran, that's nonsense, an' nothing else. Near sixty? Oh, by my purty, that's runnin' away wid the story entirely! No, nor thirty. Faith, I know them that's not more nor five or six an' twenty, that ud be glad to borry the loan of your face for a while. Divil a word o' lie in that."

"No, no, Phelim, *aroon;* I seen the day; but that's past. I remimber when the people did say I was worth lookin' at. Won't you sit near the fire? You're in the dhraft there."

"Thank you kindly, ma'am. Faith, you have the name, far an' near, for bein' the civillist woman alive this day. But, upon my sowl, if you wor ten times as civil, an' say that you're not aquil to any young girl in the parish, I'd dispute it wid you, an' say it was nothin' else than a bounce."

"*Arrah,* Phelim darlin', how can you palaver me that way? I hope your dacent father's well, Phelim, an' your honest mother?"

"Divil a fear o' them. Now, I'd hould nine to one that the purtiest o' them hasn't a sweeter mout' than you have. By dad you have—by dad you have a pair o' lips, God bless them, that—well, well——"

Phelim here ogled her with looks particularly wistful.

"Phelim, you're losin' the little senses you had."

"Faix, an' it's you that's taken them out o' me, then. A purty woman always makes a fool o' me. Divil a word o' lie in it. Faix, Mrs. Doran, ma'am, you have a chin o' your own! Well, well! Oh, begorra, I wish I hadn't come out this mornin', anyhow!"

"*Arrah,* why, Phelim? In throth it's you that's the quare Phelim!"

"Why, ma'am—Oh, bedad, it's a folly to talk. I can't go widout tastin' them. Sich a pair o' timptations as your lips, barrin' your eyes, I didn't see this many a day."

"Tastin' what, you mad crathur?"

"Why, I'll show you what I'd like to be afther tastin'. Oh, bedad, I'll have no refusin'; a purty woman always makes a foo——"

"Keep away, Phelim—keep off—bad end to you. What do you mane? Don't you see Fool Art lyin' in the corner there undher the sacks? I don't think he's asleep."

"Fool Art! why, the misfortunate idiot, what about him? Sure, he hasn't sinse to know the right hand from the left. Bedad, ma'am, the thruth is that a purty woman always makes a——"

"Throth an' you won't," said she, struggling.

"Throth an' I will, thin, taste the same lips, or we'll see who's strongest!"

A good-humoured struggle took place between the housekeeper and Phelim, who found her, in point of personal strength, very near a match for him. She laughed heartily, but Phelim attempted to salute her with a face of mock gravity as nearly resembling that of a serious man as he could assume. In the meantime, chairs were overturned and wooden dishes trundled about; a crash was heard here, and another there. Phelim drove her to the hob, and from the hob they bounced into the fire, the embers and ashes of which were kicked up into a cloud about them.

"Phelim, spare your strinth," said the funny housekeeper; "it won't do. Be asy now, or I'll get angry. The priest, too, will hear the noise, and so will Fool Art."

"To the divil wid Fool Art, an' the priest, too," said Phelim; "who cares a buckey[1] about the priest whin a purty woman like you is consarn——"

"What's this?" said the priest, stepping down from the parlour—"what's the matter? Oh, oh, upon my word, Mrs. Doran! Very good, indeed! Under my own roof, too! An'

[1] A small marble.

36

pray, ma'am, who is the gallant? Turn round, young man. Yes, I see! Why, better and better! Bouncing Phelim O'Toole, that never spoke truth! I think, Mr. O'Toole, that when you come a-courting, you ought to consider it worth while to appear somewhat more smooth in your habiliments. I simply venture to give that as my opinion."

"Why, sure enough," replied Phelim, without a moment's hesitation, "your reverence has found us out."

"Found you out! Why, is that the tone you speak in?"

"Faith, sir, thruth's best. I wanted her to tell it to you long ago, but she wouldn't. Howsomever, it's still time enough. Hem!—the thruth, sir, is that Mrs. Doran an' I is goin' to get the words said as soon as we can; so, sir, wid the help o' goodness I came to see if your reverence ud call us next Sunday wid a blessin'."

Mrs. Doran had for at least a dozen round years before this been in a state of hopelessness upon the subject of matrimony —nothing in the shape of a proposal having in the course of that period come in her way. Now we have Addison's authority for affirming that an old woman who permits the thoughts of love to get into her head becomes a very odd kind of animal. Mrs. Doran, to do her justice, had not thought of it for nearly three lustres; for this reason, that she had so far overcome her vanity as to deem it impossible that a proposal could be ever made to her. It is difficult, however, to know what a day may bring forth. Here was an offer dropping like a ripe plum into her mouth. She turned the matter over in her mind with a quickness equal to that of Phelim himself. One leading thought struck her forcibly: if she refused to close with this offer, she would never get another.

"Is it come to this, Mrs. Doran?" inquired the priest.

"Oh, bedad, sir, she knows it is," replied Phelim, giving her a wink with the safe eye.

Now Mrs. Doran began to have her suspicions. The wink she considered as decidedly ominous. Phelim, she concluded with all the sagacity of a woman thinking upon that subject, had winked at her to assent only for the purpose of getting themselves out of the scrape for the present. She feared that Phelim would be apt to break off the match, and take

37

some opportunity, before Sunday should arrive, of preventing the priest from calling them. Her decision, however, was soon made. She resolved, if possible, to pin down Phelim to his own proposal.

"Is this true, Mrs. Doran?" inquired the priest a second time.

Mrs. Doran could not, with any regard to the delicacy of her sex, give an assent without proper emotion. She accordingly applied her gown-tail to her eyes, and shed a few natural tears in reply to the affecting query of the pastor.

Phelim, in the meantime, began to feel mystified. Whether Mrs. Doran's tears were a proof that she was disposed to take the matter seriously, or whether they were tears of shame and vexation for having been caught in the character of a romping old hoyden, he could not then exactly decide. He had, however, awful misgivings upon the subject.

"Then," said the priest, "it is to be understood that I'm to call you both on Sunday?"

"There's no use in keepin' it back from you," replied Mrs. Doran. "I know it's foolish of me; but we have all our failins, and to be fond of Phelim, there, is mine. Your reverence *is* to call us next Sunday, as Phelim tould you. I am sure I can't tell you how he deluded me at all, the desaver o' the world!"

Phelim's face during this acknowledgment was, like Goldsmith's Haunch of Venison, "a subject for painters to study." His eyes projected like a hare's, until nothing could be seen but the balls. Even the drooping lid raised itself up, as if it were never to droop again.

"Well," said the priest, "I shall certainly not use a single argument to prevent you. Your choice, I must say, does you credit, particularly when it is remembered that you have come at least to years of discretion. Indeed, many persons might affirm that you have gone beyond them; but I say nothing. In the meantime your wishes must be complied with. I will certainly call Phelim O'Toole and Bridget Doran on Sunday next; and one thing I know, that we shall have a very merry congregation."

Phelim's eyes turned upon the priest and the old woman alternately with an air of bewilderment which, had the

38

priest been a man of much observation, might have attracted his attention.

"Oh, murdher alive, Mrs. Doran," said Phelim, "how am I to do for clothes? Faith, I'd like to appear dacent in the thing, anyhow."

"True," said the priest. "Have you made no provision for smoothing the externals of your admirer? Is he to appear in this trim?"

"Bedad, sir," said Phelim, "we never thought o' that. All the world knows, your reverence, that I might carry my purse in my eye an' never feel a mote in it. But the thruth is, sir, she was so lively on the subject—in a kind of pleasant, coaxin' hurry of her own—an' indeed I was so myself too. Augh, Mrs. Doran! Begorra, sir, she put her *comedher* an me entirely, so she did. Well, be my sowl, I'll be the flower of a husband to her, anyhow. I hope your reverence 'ill come to the christ'nin'? But about the clo'es?—bad luck saize the tack I have to put to my back but what you see an me, if we were to be married to-morrow."

"Well, Phelim, *aroon*," said Mrs. Doran, "his reverence here has my little pences o' money in his hands, an' the best way is for you to get the price of a suit from him. You must get clo'es, an' good ones too, Phelim, sooner nor any stop should be put to our marriage."

"Augh, Mrs. Doran," said Phelim, ogling her from the safe eye with a tender suavity of manner that did honour to his heart; "begorra, ma'am, you've played the puck entirely wid me. Faith, I'm getting fonder an' fonder of her every minute, your reverence."

He set his eye, as he uttered this, so sweetly and significantly upon the old housekeeper that the priest thought it a transgression of decorum in his presence.

"I think," said he, "you had better keep your melting looks to yourself, Phelim. Restrain your gallantry, if you please, at least until I withdraw."

"Why, blood alive! sir, when people's fond of one another it's hard to keep the love down. Augh, Mrs. Doran!—faith, you've rendhered my heart like a lump o' tallow."

"Follow me to the parlour," said the priest, "and let me

39

know, Bridget, what sum I am to give this melting gallant of yours."

"I may as well get what'll do the weddin' at wanst," observed Phelim. "It'll save throuble, in the first place; an' sackinly, it'll save time; for, plase goodness, I'll have everything ready for houldin' the weddin' the Monday afther the last call. By the hole o' my coat, the minute I get the clo'es we'll be spliced, an' then for the honeymoon!"

"How much money shall I give him?" said the priest.

"Indeed, sir, I think you ought to know that; I'm ignorant of what ud make a dacent weddin'. We don't intend to get marrid undher a hedge; we've frinds on both sides, an' of coorse we must have them about us, plase goodness."

"Begorra, sir, it's no wondher I'm fond of her, the darlin'! Bad win to you, Mrs. Doran, how did you come over me at all?"

"Bridget," said the priest, "I have asked you a simple question, to which I expect a plain answer. What money am I to give this tallow-hearted swain of yours?"

"Why, your reverence, whatsomever you think may be enough for full, an' plinty, an' dacency at the weddin'."

"Not forgettin' the thatch for me, in the manetime," said Phelim. "Nothin' less will sarve us, plase your reverence. Maybe, sir, you'd think of comin' to the weddin' yourself?"

"There are in my hands," observed the priest, "one hundred and twenty-two guineas of your money, Bridget. Here, Phelim, are ten for your wedding suit and wedding expenses. Go to your wedding? No! don't suppose for a moment that I countenance this transaction in the slightest degree. I comply with your wishes, but I heartily despise you both—but certainly this foolish old woman most. Give me an acknowledgment for this, Phelim."

"God bless you, sir!" said Phelim, as if he had paid them a compliment. "In regard o' the acknowledgment, sir, I acknowledge it wid all my heart; but bad luck to the scrape at all I can write."

"Well, no matter. You admit, Bridget, that I give this money to this blessed youth by your authority and consent."

"Surely, your reverence; I'll never go back of it."

"Now, Phelim," said the priest, "you have the money; pray get married as soon as possible."

"I'll give you my oath," said Phelim; "an' be the blessed iron tongs in the grate there, I'll not lose a day in getting myself spliced. Isn't she the tendher-hearted sowl, your reverence? Augh, Mrs. Doran!"

"Leave my place," said the priest. "I cannot forget the old proverb, that one fool makes many, but an old fool is worse than any. So it is with this old woman."

"Ould woman! Oh, thin, I'm sure I don't desarve this from your reverence!" exclaimed the housekeeper, wiping her eyes. "If I'm a little seasoned now, you know I wasn't always so. If ever there was a faithful sarvant, I was that, and managed your house and place as honestly as I'll manage my own, plase goodness."

As they left the parlour Phelim became the consoler.

"Whisht, you darlin'!" he exclaimed. "Sure, you'll have Bouncin' Phelim to comfort you. But now that he has shut the door, what—hem—I'd take it as a piece o' civility if you'd open my eyes a little; I mane—hem—was it—is this doin' him—or how?' Are you—hem—do you undherstand me, Mrs. Doran?"

"What is it you want to know, Phelim? I think everything is very plain."

"Oh, the divil a plainer, I suppose. But, in the mane-time, might one ax, out o' mere curiosity, if you're in arnest?"

"In arnest! Arrah, what did I give you my money for, Phelim? Well, now that everything is settled, God forgive you if you make a bad husband to me."

"A bad what?"

"I say, God forgive you if you make a bad husband to me. I'm afeard, Phelim, that I'll be too foolish about you—that I'll be too fond of you."

Phelim looked at her in solemn silence, and then replied: "Let us trust in God that you may be enabled to overcome the weakness. Pray to Him to avoid all folly, an', above everything, to give you a dacent stock of discration, for it's a mighty fine thing for a woman of your yea——hem, a mighty fine thing it is, indeed, for a sasoned woman, as you say you are."

" When will the weddin' take place, Phelim ? "

" The what ? " said Phelim, opening his brisk eye with a fresh stare of dismay.

" Why, the weddin', *acushla*. When will it take place ? I think the Monday afther the last call ud be the best time. We wouldn't lose a day thin. Throth, I long to hear my last call over, Phelim, jewel."

Phelim gave her another look.

" The last call ! Thin, by the vestment, you don't long half as much for your last call as I do."

" *Arrah*, Phelim, did you take the—the—what you wor wantin' a while agone ? Throth, myself disremimbers."

" Ay, a round dozen o' them. How can you forget it ? "

The idiot in the corner here gave a loud snore, but composed himself to sleep, as if insensible to all that passed.

" Throth, an' I do forget it. Now, Phelim, you'll not go till you take a cup o' tay wid myself. Throth, I do forget it, Phelim darlin', jewel."

Phelim's face now assumed a very queer expression. He twisted his features into all possible directions; brought his mouth first round to one ear and then to the other; put his hand, as if in great pain, on the pit of his stomach; lifted one knee up till it almost touched his chin, then let it down, and instantly brought up the other in a similar manner.

" Phelim darlin', what ails you ? " inquired the tender old nymph. " *Wurrah*, man alive, aren't you well ? "

" Oh, be the vestment," said Phelim, " what's this at all ! Murdher *sheery*, what'll I do ! Oh, I'm very bad ! At death's door, so I am ! Begorra, Mrs. Doran, I must be off ! "

" *Wurrah*, Phelim dear, won't you stop till we settle everything ? "

" Oh, purshuin' to the hap'orth I can settle till I recover o' this murdherin' colic ! All's asthray wid me in the inside. I'll see you—I'll see you—*Hanim un diouol !* what's this—I must be off like a shot—oh, murdher *sheery !*—but—but—I'll see you to-morrow. In the manetime, I'm—I'm for ever oblaged to you for—for—lendin' me the—loan of—oh, by the vestments, I'm a gone man !—for lendin' me the loan of the ten guineas—Oh, I'm gone ! "

Phelim disappeared on uttering these words, and his strides

on passing out of the house were certainly more rapid and vigorous than those of a man labouring under pain. In fact, he never looked behind him until one-half the distance between the priest's house and his father's cabin had been fairly traversed.

Some misgivings occurred to the old housekeeper, but her vanity, having been revived by Phelim's blarney, would not permit her to listen to them. She had, besides, other motives to fortify her faith in his attachment. First, there was her money, a much larger sum than ever Phelim could expect with any other woman, young or old; again, they were to be called on the following Sunday, and she knew that when a marriage affair proceeds so far, obstruction or disappointment is not to be apprehended.

When Phelim reached home he found the father returned after having borrowed a full suit of clothes for him. Sam Appleton, on hearing from Larry that Bouncing Phelim was about to get a " great match," generously lent him coat, waistcoat, hat, and small-clothes.

When Phelim presented himself at home he scarcely replied to the queries put to him by his father and mother concerning his interview with the priest. He sat down, rubbed his hands, scratched his head, rose up, and walked to and fro, in a mood of mind so evidently between mirth and chagrin that his worthy parents knew not whether to be merry or miserable.

" Phelim," said the mother, " did you take anything while you wor away?"

" Did I take anything, is it? *Arrah*, be asy, old woman! Did I take anything? Faith, you may say that!"

" Let us know, anyhow, what's the matther wid you?" asked the father.

" Tare-an'-ounze!" exclaimed the son, " what is this for at all, at all? It's too killin' I am, so it is."

" You're not lockin' at Sam Appleton's clo'es," said the father, " that he lent you the loan of, hat an' all."

" Do you want to put an affront upon me, ould man? To the divil wid himself an' his clo'es! When I want clo'es I'll buy them wid my own money!"

" Larry," observed the mother, " there's yourself all over —as proud as a paycock when the sup's in his head, an' ud

43

spake as big widout the sign o' money in your pocket as if you had the rint of an estate."

"What do you say about the sign o' money?" exclaimed Phelim, with a swagger. "Maybe you'll call that the sign o' money!" he added, producing the ten guineas in gold.

The father and mother looked at it for a considerable time, then at each other, and shook their heads.

"Phelim!" said the father solemnly.

"Phelim!" said the mother awfully; and both shook their heads again.

"You wor never over-scrupulous," the father proceeded, "an' you know you have many little things to answer for, in the way of picking up what didn't belong to yourself. I think, too, you're not the same you wor afore you tuck to swearin' the *alibis*."

"Faith an' I doubt I'll have to get some one to swear an *alibi* for myself soon," Phelim replied.

"Why, blessed hour!" said Larry, "didn't I often tell you never to join the boys in anything that might turn out a hangin' matther?"

"If this is not a hangin' matther," said Phelim, "it's something nearly as bad—it's a marryin' matther. Sure, I deluded another since you seen me last. Divil a word o' lie in it. I was clane fell in love wid this mornin' about seven o'clock."

"But how did you get the money, Phelim?"

"Why, from the youthful sprig that fell in love wid me. Sure, we're to be 'called' in the chapel on Sunday next."

"Why, thin, now, Phelim! An' who is the young crathur? for in throth she must be young to go to give the money beforehand!"

"Murdher!" exclaimed Phelim, "what's this for? Hell purshue her, the ould rat-thrap! Was ever any one done as I am! Who is she? Why she's—oh, murdher, oh!—she's no other than—hem!—divil a one else than Father O'Hara's housekeeper, ould Biddy Doran!"

The mirth of the old couple was excessive. The father laughed till he fell off his stool, and the mother till the tears ran down her cheeks.

"Death alive, ould man! but you're very merry," said Phelim. "If you wor my age, an' in such an amplush, you'd laugh on the wrong side o' your mouth. Maybe you'll turn your tune when you hear that she has a hundher an' twenty guineas."

"An' you'll be rich, too," said the father. "The sprig an' you will be rich !—ha, ha, ha ! "

"An' the family they'll have ! " said the mother, in convulsions.

"Why, in regard o' that," said Phelim, rather nettled, "sure, we can do as my father an' you did : we can kiss the Lucky Stone, an' make a station."

"Phelim, *aroon*," said the mother seriously, "put it out o' your head. Sure, you wouldn't go to bring me a daughter-in-law oulder nor myself ? "[1]

"I'd as soon go over,"[1] said Phelim, "or swing itself, before I'd marry sich a piece o' desate. Hard feedin' to her ! how she did me to my face ! "

Phelim then entered into a long-visaged detail of the scene at Father O'Hara's, dwelling bitterly on the alacrity with which the old housekeeper ensnared him in his own mesh.

"However," he concluded, "she'd be a sharp one if she'd do me altogether. We're not marrid yet; an' I've a consate o' my own that she's done for the ten guineas, anyhow ! "

A family counsel was immediately held upon Phelim's matrimonial prospects. On coming close to the speculation of Miss Patterson, it was somehow voted, notwithstanding Phelim's powers of attraction, to be rather a discouraging one. Gracey Dalton was also given up. The matter was now serious, the time short, and Phelim's bounces touching his own fascinations with the sex in general were considerably abated. It was therefore resolved that he ought to avail himself of Sam Appleton's clothes until his own could be made. Sam, he said, would not press him for them immediately, inasmuch as he was under obligation to Phelim's silence upon some midnight excursions that he had made.

"Not," added Phelim, "but I'm as much, an' maybe more, in his power than he is in mine."

When breakfast was over, Phelim and the father, after having determined to "drink a bottle" that night in the

---

[1] A familiar term for "transportation."

family of a humble young woman, named Donovan, who, they all agreed, would make an excellent wife for him, rested upon their oars until evening. In the meantime Phelim sauntered about the village, as he was in the habit of doing, whilst the father kept the day as a holiday. We have never told our readers that Phelim was in love, because, in fact, we know not whether he was or not. Be this as it may, we simply inform them that in a little shed in the lower end of the village lived a person with whom Phelim was very intimate, called Foodle Flattery. He was, indeed, a man after Phelim's own heart, and Phelim was a boy after his. He maintained himself by riding country races; by handling, breeding, and feeding cocks; by fishing, poaching, and serving processes; and finally, by his knowledge as a cow-doctor and farrier— into the two last of which he had given Phelim some insight. We say the two last, for in most of the other accomplishments Phelim was fully his equal. Phelim frequently envied him his life. It was an idle, amusing, vagabond kind of existence, just such a one as he felt a relish for. This man had a daughter, rather well-looking; and it so happened that he and Phelim had frequently spent whole nights out together, no one knew on what employment. Into Flattery's house did Phelim saunter with something like an inclination to lay the events of the day before him, and to ask his advice upon his future prospects. On entering the cabin he was much surprised to find the daughter in a very melancholy mood; a circumstance which puzzled him not a little, as he knew that they lived very harmoniously together. Sally had been very useful to her father, and if fame did not belie her, was some- times worthy Foodle's assistant in his nocturnal exploits. She was certainly reputed to be "light-handed"; an imputation which caused the young men of her acquaintance to avoid, in their casual conversations with her, any allusion to matrimony.

"Sally, *achora*," said Phelim, when he saw her in distress, "what's the fun? Where's your father?"

"Oh, Phelim," she replied, bursting into tears, "long runs the fox, but he's cotch at last. My father's in gaol."

Phelim's jaw dropped. "In gaol! *Chorp an diowol*, no!"

"It's thruth, Phelim. Curse upon this Whiteboy business; I wish it had never come into the counthry at all."

46

"Sally, I must see him; you know I must. But tell me how it happened. Was it at home he was taken?"

"No; he was taken this mornin' in the market. I was wid him sellin' some chickens. What'll you and Sam Appleton do, Phelim?"

"Uz! Why, what danger is there aither to Sam or me, you darlin'?"

"I'm sure, Phelim, I don't know; but he tould me that if I was provided for he'd be firm, an' take chance of his thrial. But he says, poor man, that it ud break his heart to be thransported, lavin' me behind him wid nobody to take care o' me. He says, too, if anything 'ud make him stag,[1] it's fear of the thrial goin' aginst himself; for, as he said to me, 'what ud become of you, Sally, if anything happened me?'"

A fresh flood of tears followed this disclosure, and Phelim's face, which was certainly destined to undergo on that day many variations of aspect, became remarkably blank.

"Sally, you insinivator, I'll hould a thousand guineas you'd never guess what brought me here to-day."

"Arrah, how could I, Phelim? To plan somethin' wid my fadher, maybe."

"No, but to plan somethin' wid yourself, you coaxin' jewel, you. Now tell me this—Would you marry a certain gay, roguish, well-built young fellow they call Bouncin' Phelim?"

"Phelim, don't be gettin' an wid your fun now, an' me in affliction. Sure, I know well you wouldn't throw yourself away on a poor girl like me, that has nothing but a good pair of hands to live by."

"Be my sowl, an' you live by them. Well, but set in case—supposin'—that same Bouncin' Phelim was willin' to make you mistress of the half acre, what ud you be sayin'?"

"Phelim, if a body thought you worn't jokin' them—Ah, the dickens go wid you, Phelim—this is more o' your thricks —But if it was thruth you wor spakin', Phelim?"

"It is thruth," said Phelim; "be the vestment, it's nothin'

---

[1] Inform.

else. Now, say yes or no; for if it's a thing that it's to be a match, you must go an' tell him that I'll marry you, an' he must be as firm as a rock. But see—Sally, by thim five crasses, it's not bekase your father's in I'm marryin' you at all. Sure, I'm in love wid you, *acushla!* Divil a lie in it. Now, yes or no?"

"Well—throth—to be sure—the sorra one, Phelim, but you have quare ways wid you. Now, are you downright in airnest?"

"Be the stool I'm sittin' on!"

"Well, in the name o' goodness, I'll go to my father an' let him know it. Poor man, it'll take the fear out of his heart. Now, can he depind on you, Phelim?"

"Why, all I can say is that we'll get ourselves called on Sunday next. Let himself, sure, send some one to autorise the priest to call us. An' now that all's settled, don't I desarve somethin'? Oh, begorra, surely."

"Behave, Phelim—oh—oh—Phelim, now—there, you've tuck it—och, the curse of the crows on you, see the way you have my hair down! There now, you broke my comb too. Throth, you're a wild slip, Phelim. I hope you won't be goin' on this a-way wid the girls when you get married."

"Is it me, you coaxer? No; faith, I'll wear a pair of winkers, for 'fraid o' lookin' at them at all. Oh, begorra, no, Sally; I'll lave that to the great people. Sure, they say, the devil a differ they make at all."

"Go off now, Phelim, till I get ready and set out to my father. But, Phelim, never breathe a word about him bein' in gaol. No one knows it but ourselves—that is none o' the neighbours."

"I'll sing dumb," said Phelim. "Well, *banaght lath a rogorah!* Tell him the thruth—to be game, and he'll find you and me sweeled together whin he comes out, plase goodness."

Phelim was but a few minutes gone when the old military cap of Fool Art projected from the little bedroom, which a wicker wall, plastered with mud, divided from the other part of the cabin.

"Is he gone?" said Art.

"You may come out, Art," said she, "he's gone."

"Ha!" said Art triumphantly, "I often tould him, when he vexed me an' pelted me wid snowballs, that I'd come 'long sides wid him yet. An' it's not over aither. Fool Art can snore when he's not asleep, an' see wid his eyes shut. Wherroo for Art!"

"But, Art, maybe he intinds to marry the housekeeper afther all?"

"Hi the colic, the colic!
An' ho the colic for Phelim!"

"Then you think he won't, Art?"

"Hi the colic, the colic!
An' ho the colic for Phelim!"

"Now, Art, don't say a word about my father not bein' in gaol. He's to be back from my grandfather's in a short time, an' if we manage well, you'll see what you'll get, Art —a brave new shirt, Art."

"Art has the lane for Phelim, but it's not the long one wid no turn in it. Wherroo for Art!"

Phelim, on his return home, felt queer. Here was a second matrimonial predicament, considerably worse than the first, into which he was hooked decidedly against his will. The worst feature in this case was the danger to be apprehended from Foodle Flattery's disclosures, should he take it into his head to peach upon his brother Whiteboys. Indeed, Phelim began to consider it a calamity that he ever entered into their system at all; for on running over his exploits along with them, he felt that he was liable to be taken up any morning of the week and lodged in one of his Majesty's boarding-houses. The only security he had was the honesty of his confederates; and experience took the liberty of pointing out to him many cases in which those who considered themselves quite secure upon the same grounds either dangled or crossed the water. He remembered, too, some prophecies that had been uttered concerning him with reference both to hanging and matrimony. Touching the former, it was often said that "he'd die where the bird flies" —between heaven and earth; on matrimony, that there seldom was a swaggerer among the girls but came to the ground at last.

Now, Phelim had a memory of his own, and in turning over his situation, and the prophecies that had been so confidently pronounced concerning him, he felt, as we said, rather queer. He found his father and mother in excellent spirits when he got home. The good man had got a gallon of whisky on credit; for it had been agreed on not to break the ten golden guineas until they should have ascertained how the match-making would terminate that night at Donovan's.

"Phelim," said the father, "strip yourself, an' put on Sam's clo'es; you must send him down yours for a day or two; he says it's the least he may have the wearin' o' them, so long as you have his."

"Right enough," said Phelim; "wid all my heart. I'm ready to make a fair swap wid him any day, for that matther."

"I sent word to the Donovans that we're to go to coort there to-night," said Larry, "so that they'll be prepared for us; an' as it would be shabby not to have a friend, I asked Sam Appleton himself. He's to folly us."

"I see," said Phelim, "I see. Well, the best boy in Europe Sam is for sich a spree. Now, fadher, you must lie like the ould *diouol* to-night. Back everything I say, an' there's no fear of us. But about what she's to get, you must hould out for that. I'm to despise it, you know. I'll abuse you for spakin' about fortune, but don't budge an inch."

"It's not the first time I've done that for you, Phelim; but in regard o' these ten guineas, why, you must put them in your pocket, for 'fraid they'd be wantin' to get off wid layin' down guinea for guinea. You see, they don't think we have a rap; an' if they propose it, we'll be up to them."

"Larry," observed Sheelah, "don't make a match, except they give that pig they have. Hould out for that by all means."

"Tare-an'-ounze!" exclaimed Phelim, "am I goin' to take the counthry out o' the face? By the vestments, I'm a purty boy! Do you know the fresh news I have for yees?"

"Not ten guineas more, Phelim," replied the father.

"Maybe you soodhered another ould woman," said the mother.

"Be asy," replied Phelim. "No, but by the five crasses, I deluded a young one since I went out!"

The old couple were once more disposed to be mirthful, but Phelim confirmed his assertion with such a multiplicity of oaths that they believed him. Nothing, however, could wring the secret of her name out of him. He had reasons for concealing it which he did not wish to divulge. In fact, he could never endure ridicule, and the name of Sally Flattery as the person whom he had "deluded," would constitute on his part a triumph quite as sorry as that which he had achieved in Father O'Hara's. In Ireland no man ever thinks of marrying a female thief—which Sally was strongly suspected to be —except some worthy fellow who happens to be gifted with the same propensity.

When the proper hour arrived, honest Phelim, after having already made arrangements to be called on the following Sunday as the intended husband of two females, now proceeded with great coolness to make, if possible, a similar engagement with a third.

There is something, however, to be said for Phelim. His conquest over the housekeeper was considerably out of the common course of love affairs. He had drawn upon his invention only to bring himself and the old woman out of the ridiculous predicament in which the priest found them. He had, moreover, intended to prevail on her to lend him the hat, in case the priest himself had refused him. He was consequently not prepared for the vigorous manner in which Mrs. Doran fastened upon the subject of matrimony. On suspecting that she was inclined to be serious, he pleaded his want of proper apparel; but here again the liberality of the housekeeper silenced him, whilst, at the same time, it opened an excellent prospect of procuring that which he most required—a decent suit of clothes. This induced him to act a part that he did not feel. He saw the old woman was resolved to outwit him, and he resolved to overreach the old woman.

His marriage with Sally Flattery was to be merely a matter of chance. If he married her at all, he knew it must be in self-defence. He felt that her father had him in his power, and that he was anything but a man to be depended on. He

51

also thought that his being called with her on the Sunday following would neutralise his call with the housekeeper; just as positive and negative quantities in algebra cancel each other. But he was quite ignorant that the story of Flattery's imprisonment was merely a plan of the daughter's to induce him to marry her.

With respect to Peggy Donovan, he intended, should he succeed in extricating himself from the meshes which the other two had thrown around him, that she should be the elected one to whom he was anxious to unite himself. As to the confusion produced by being called to three at once, he knew that, however laughable in itself, it would be precisely something like what the parish would expect from him. Bouncing Phelim was no common man, and to be called to three on the same Sunday would be a corroboration of his influence with the sex. It certainly chagrined him not a little that one of them was an old woman, and the other of indifferent morals, but still it exhibited the claim of three women upon one man, and that satisfied him. His mode of proceeding with Peggy Donovan was regular, and according to the usages of the country. The notice had been given that he and his father would go a-courting, and of course they brought the whisky with them, that being the custom among persons in their circumstances in life. These humble courtships very much resemble the driving of a bargain between two chapmen; for, indeed, the closeness of the demands on the one side, and the reluctance of concession on the other, are almost incredible. Many a time has a match been broken up by a refusal on the one part to give a slip of a pig, or a pair of blankets, or a year-old calf. These are small matters in themselves, but they are of importance to those who perhaps have nothing else on earth with which to begin the world.

The house to which Phelim and his father directed themselves was, like their own, of the humblest description. The floor of it was about sixteen feet by twelve; its furniture rude and scanty. To the right of the fire was a bed, the four posts of which ran up to the low roof; it was curtained with straw mats, with the exception of an opening about a foot and a half wide on the side next the fire, through which those who slept in it passed. A little below the foot of the bed were ranged a few shelves of deal, supported by pins of wood driven into the wall. These constituted the dresser. In the lower end of the house stood a potato-bin, made up of stakes driven into the floor, and wrought with strong wicker-work. Tied to another stake beside this bin stood a cow, whose hinder part projected so close to the door that those who entered the cabin were compelled to push her over out of their way. This, indeed, was effected without much difficulty, for the animal became so habituated to the necessity of moving aside, that it was only necessary to lay the hand upon her. Above the door in the inside, almost touching the roof, was the hen-roost, made also of wickerwork; and opposite the bed, on the other side of the fire, stood a meal-chest, its lid on a level with a little pane of glass which served as a window. An old straw chair, a few stools, a couple of pots, some wooden vessels and crockery, completed the furniture of the house. The pig to which Sheelah alluded was not kept within the cabin, that filthy custom being now altogether obsolete.

This catalogue of cottage furniture may appear to our English readers very miserable. We beg them to believe, however, that if every cabin in Ireland were equally comfortable, the country would be comparatively happy. Still it is to be remembered that the *dramatis personæ* of our story are of the humblest class.

When seven o'clock drew nigh, the inmates of this little cabin placed themselves at a clear fire; the father on one side, the mother at the other, and the daughter directly between them, knitting, for this is usually the occupation of a female on such a night. Everything in the house was clear, the floor swept, the ashes removed from the hearth, the parents in their best clothes, and the daughter also in her holiday apparel. She was a plain girl, neither remarkable for beauty nor otherwise. Her eyes, however, were good, so were her teeth, and an anxious look, produced of course by an occasion so interesting to a female, heightened her complexion to a blush that became her. The creature had certainly made the most of her little finery. Her face shone like that of a child after a fresh scrubbing with a strong towel; her hair, carefully curled with the hot blade of a knife, had been smoothed with soap until it became lustrous by repeated polishing, and her best red ribbon was tied tightly about it in a smart knot, that stood out on the side of her head with something of a coquettish air. Old Donovan and his wife maintained a conversation upon some indifferent subject, but the daughter evidently paid little attention to what they said. It being near the hour appointed for Phelim's arrival, she sat with an appearance of watchful trepidation, occasionally listening, and starting at every sound that she thought bore any resemblance to a man's voice or footstep.

At length the approach of Phelim and his father was announced by a verse of a popular song, for singing which Phelim was famous.

> " 'A sailor coorted a farmer's daughter
> That lived contagious to the Isle of Man.
> A long time coortin', an' still discoorsin'
> Of things consarnin' the ocean wide;
> At linth he saize, " Me own dearest darlint,
> Will you consint for to be me bride ?" ' "

" An' so she did consint, the darlin'; but what the puck would she do else ? God save the family ! Paddy Donovan, how is your health ? Molly, *avourneen*, I'm glad to hear that you're thrivin'. An' Peggy — eh ! Ah, begorra, fadher, here's somethin' to look at ! Give us the hand of you, you bloomer ! Och, och ! faith, you're the daisy ! "

" Phelim," said the father, " will you behave yourself ? Haven't you the night before you for your capers. Paddy Donovan, I'm glad to see you ! Molly, give us your right hand, for, in throth, I have a regard for you ! Peggy dear, how are you ? But I'm sure I needn't be axin' when I look at you ! In throth, Phelim, she is somethin' to throw your eye at."

" Larry Toole, you're welcome," replied Donovan and his wife, " an' so is your son. Take stools, both of you, an' draw near the hearth. Here, Phelim," said the latter, " draw in an' sit beside myself."

" Thank you kindly, Molly," replied Phelim ; " but I'll do

no sich thing. *Arrah,* do you think, now, that I'd begin to gosther wid an ould woman, while I have the likes o' Peggy, the darlin', beside me ? I'm up to a thrick worth nine of it. No, no; this chest 'll do. Sure, you know, I must help the ' duck of diamonds ' here to count her stitches."

" Paddy," said Larry, in a friendly whisper, " put this whisky past for a while, barrin' this bottle that we must taste for good luck. Sam Appleton's to come up afther us, an' I suppose some o' your own *cleaveens* 'ill be here afther a while."

" Thrue for you," said Donovan. " Jemmy Burn and Antony Devlin is to come over presently. But, Larry, this is nonsense. One bottle o' whisky was lashins; my goodness, what'll we be doin' wid a whole gallon ? "

" Dacency or nothin', Paddy ; if it was my last I'd show sperit, an' why not ? Who'd be for the shabby thing ? "

" Well, well, Larry, I can't say but you're right, afther all ! Maybe I'd do the same thing myself, for all I'm spakin' aginst it."

The old people then passed round an introductory glass, after which they chatted away for an hour or so, somewhat like the members of a committee who talk upon indifferent topics until their brethren are all assembled.

Phelim, in the meantime, grappled with the daughter, whose knitting he spoiled by hooking the thread with his finger, jogging her elbow until he ran the needles past each other, and finally unravelling her clue ; all which she bore with great good-humour. Sometimes, indeed, she ventured to give him a thwack upon the shoulder, with a laughing frown upon her countenance, in order to correct him for teasing her.

When Jemmy Burn and Antony Devlin arrived, the spirits of the party got up. The whisky was formally produced, but as yet the subject of the courtship, though perfectly under-stood, was not introduced. Phelim and the father were anxious to await the presence of Sam Appleton, who was considered, by the way, a first-rate hand at match-making.

Phelim, as is the wont, on finding the din of the conversation raised to the proper pitch, stole one of the bottles, and prevailed on Peggy to adjourn with him to the potato-bin. Here they ensconced themselves very snugly ; but not, as might be supposed, contrary to the knowledge and consent of the seniors, who winked at each other on seeing Phelim gallantly tow her down with the bottle under his arm. It was only the common usage on such occasions, and not considered any violation whatsoever of decorum. When Phelim's prior engagements are considered, it must be admitted that there was something singularly ludicrous in the humorous look he gave over his shoulder at the company as he went toward the bin, having the bottom of the whisky bottle projecting behind his elbow, winking at them in return, by way of a hint to mind their own business and allow him to plead for himself. The bin, however, turned out to be rather an uneasy seat, for as the potatoes lay in a slanting heap against the wall, Phelim and his sweetheart were perpetually sliding down from the top to the bottom. Phelim could be industrious when it suited his pleasure. In a few minutes those who sat about the fire imagined, from the noise at the bin, that the house was about to come about their ears.

"Phelim, you thief," said the father, "what's all that noise for?"

"*Chrosh orrin!*" said Molly Donovan, "is that tundher?"

"Devil carry these piatees," exclaimed Phelim, raking them down with both hands and all his might, "if there's any sittin' at all upon them! I'm levellin' them to prevint Peggy, the darlin', from slidderin', an' to give us time to be talkin' somethin' lovin' to one another. The curse o' Cromwell an them! One might as well dhrink a glass o' whisky wid his sweetheart, or spake a tindher word to her, on the wings of a windmill as here. There, now they're as level as you plase, *acushla!* Sit down, you jewel, you, an' give me the egg-shell, till we have a sup o' the crathur in comfort. Faith, it was too soon for us to be comin' down in the world!"

Phelim and Peggy, having each emptied the egg-shell, which among the poorer Irish is frequently the substitute for a glass, entered into the following sentimental dialogue, which was covered by the loud and entangled conversation of their friends about the fire; Phelim's arm lovingly about her neck, and his head laid down snugly against her cheek.

"Now, Peggy, you darlin' o' the world—bad cess to me, but

I'm as glad as two tenpennies that I levelled these piatees; there was no sittin' an them. Eh, *avourneen?* "

" Why, we're comfortable now, anyhow, Phelim ! "

" Faith, you may say that "—(a loving squeeze). " Now, Peggy, begin an' tell us all about your bachelors."

" The sarra one ever I had, Phelim."

" Oh, murdher, *sheery,* what a bounce ! Bad cess to me if you can spake a word o' thruth afther that, you common desaver ! Worn't you an' Paddy Moran pullin' a coard ? "

" No, in throth ; it was given out on us, but we never wor, Phelim. Nothin' ever passed betune us but common civility. He thrated my father an' mother wanst to share of half a pint in the Lammas Fair, when I was along wid them ; but he never broke discoorse wid me, barrin', as I sed, in civility an' friendship."

" An' do you mane to put it down my throath that you never had a sweetheart at all ? "

" The nerra one."

" Oh, you thief ! Wid two sich lips o' your own, an' two sich eyes o' your own, and two sich cheeks o' your own !—oh, by the tarn, that won't pass."

" Well, an' supposin' I had—behave, Phelim—supposin' I had, where's the harm ? Sure, it's well known all the sweethearts you had, an' yet have, I suppose."

" Begorra, an' that's thruth ; an' the more the merrier, you jewel, you, till one gets marrid. I had enough o' them in my day ; but you're the flower o' them all, that I'd like to spend my life wid "—(a squeeze).

" The sarra one word the men say a body can trust. I warrant you tould that story to every one o' them as well as to me. Stop, Phelim—it's well known that what you say to the *colleens* is no gospel. You know what they christened you 'Bouncin' Phelim' for."

" Betune you an' me, Peggy, I'll tell you a sacret : I was the boy for deludin' them. It's very well known the matches I might a' got ; but you see, you little shaver, it was waitin' for yourself I was."

" For me ! A purty story, indeed ! I'm sure it was ! Oh, afther that ! Why, Phelim, how can you — Well, well, did any one ever hear the likes ? "

57

"Be the vestments, it's thruth. I had you in my eye these three years, but was waitin' till I'd get together as much money as ud set us up in the world dacently. Give me that egg-shell agin. Talkin's druthy work. *Shudorth, a rogarah!* an' a pleasant honeymoon to us!"

"Wait till we're marrid first, Phelim; thin it'll be time enough to dhrink *that.*"

"Come, *acushla,* it's your turn now; taste the shell an' you'll see how lovin' it'll make us. Mother's milk's a thrifle to it."

"Well, if I take this, Phelim, I'll not touch another dhrop to-night. In the manetime, here's whatever's best for us! Whoo! Oh, my! but that's strong! I dunna how the people can dhrink so much of it!"

"Faith, nor me; except bekase they have a regard for it, an' that it's worth havin' a regard for, jist like yourself an' me. Upon my faix, Peggy, it bates all, the love an' likin' I have for you, an' ever had these three years past. I tould you about the eyes, *mavourneen,* an'—an'—about the lips——"

"Phelim—behave—I say—now stop wid you—well—well —but you're the tazin' Phelim! Throth, the girls may be glad when you're marrid!" exclaimed Peggy, adjusting her polished hair.

"Bad cess to the bit if ever I got so sweet a one in my life—the soft end of a honeycomb's a fool to it. One thing, Peggy, I can tell you—that I'll love you in great style. Whin we're marrid it's I that'll *soodher* you up. I won't let the wind blow on you. You must give up workin' too. All I'll ax you to do will be to nurse the childher; an' that same will keep you busy enough, plase goodness."

"Upon my faix, Phelim, you're the very sarra, so you are. Will you be asy now! I'll engage when you're marrid it'll soon be another story wid you. Maybe you'd care little about us thin!"

"Be the vestments, I'm spaking pure gospel, so I am. Sure, you don't know that to be good husbands runs in our family. Every one o' them was as sweet as thracle to their wives. Why, there's that ould cock, my fadher, an' if you'd see how he butthers up the ould woman to this day, it ud make your heart warm to any man o' the family."

58

"Ould an' young was ever an' always the same to you, Phelim. Sure, the ouldest woman in the parish, if she happened to be single, couldn't miss of your blarney. It's reported you're going to be marrid to an ould woman."

"He—hem—ahem! Bad luck to this cowld I have! It's stickin' in my throath entirely, so it is!—hem!— To a what?"

"Why, to an ould woman wid a great deal o' the hard goold!"

Phelim put his hand instinctively to his waistcoat-pocket, in which he carried the housekeeper's money.

"Would you oblige one wid her name?"

"You know ould Molly Kavanagh well enough, Phelim."

Phelim put up an inward ejaculation of thanks.

"To the sarra wid her, an' all sasoned women! God be praised—that the night's fine, anyhow! Hand me the shell, and we'll take a *gauliogue* aich, an' afther that we'll begin an' talk over how lovin' an' fond o' one another we'll be."

"You're takin' too much o' the whisky, Phelim. Oh, for goodness' sake!—oh—b—b—n—now be asy. Faix, I'll go to the fire, an' lave you altogether, so I will, if you don't give over slustherin' me that way, an' stoppin' my breath."

"Here's all happiness to our two selves, *acushla machree!* Now thry another *gauliogue,* an' you'll see how deludin' it'll make you."

"Not a sup, Phelim."

"*Arrah,* nonsense! Be the vestments, it's as harmless as new milk from the cow. It'll only do you good, *alanna.* Come now, Peggy, don't be ondacent, an' it our first night's coortin'! Blood alive! don't make little o' my father's son, on sich a night, an' us at business like this, anyhow!"

"Phelim, by the crass, I won't take it; so that ends it. Do you want to make little o' me? It's not much you'd think o' me in your mind if I'd dhrink it."

"The shell's not half full."

"I wouldn't break my oath for all the whisky in the kingdom; so don't ax me. It's neither right nor proper of you to force it an me."

"Well, all I say is that it's makin' little of one Phelim O'Toole, that hasn't a thought in his body but what's over

59

head an' ears in love wid you. I must only dhrink it for you myself, thin. Here's all kinds o' good fortune to us! Now, Peggy—sit closer to me, *acushla!*—now, Peggy, are you fond o' me at all? Tell thruth now."

"Fond o' you! Sure, you know all the girls is fond of you. Aren't you 'the boy for deludin' them'?"

"Come, come, you shaver; that won't do. Be sarious. If you knew how my heart's warmin' to you this minute, you'd fall in love wid my shadow. Come, now, out wid it. Are you fond of a sartin boy not far from you, called Bouncin' Phelim?"

"To be sure I am. Are you satisfied now? Phelim! I say——"

"Faith, it won't pass, *avourneen.* That's not the voice for it. Don't you hear me, how tendher I spake wid my mouth brathin' into your ear, *acushla machree?* Now turn about, like a purty enticin' girl as you are, an' put your sweet bill to my ear the same way, an' whisper what you know into it? That's a darlin'! Will you, *achora?*"

"An' maybe all this time you're promised to another?"

"Be the vestments, I'm not promised to one. Now! Saize the one!"

"You'll say that, anyhow!"

"Do you see my hands acrass? Be thim five crasses, I'm not promised to a girl livin', so I'm not; nor wouldn't, bekase I had you in my eye. Now will you tell me what I'm wantin' of you? The grace o' heaven light down an you, an' be a good, coaxin' darlin' for wanst! Be this an' be that, if ever you heerd or seen sich doins an' times as we'll have when we're marrid! Now the *weeny* whispher, *a colleen dhas!*"

"It's time enough yet to let you know my mind, Phelim. If you behave yourself an' be—Why, thin, is it at the bottle agin you are? Now, don't dhrink so much, Phelim, or it'll get into your head. I was sayin' that if you behave yourself, an' be a good boy, I may tell you somethin' soon."

"Somethin' soon! Live horse, an' you'll get grass! Peggy, if that's the way wid you, the love's all on my side, I see clearly. Are you willin' to marry me, anyhow?"

"I'm willin' to do whatsomever my father an' mother wishes."

"I'm for havin' the weddin' off-hand; an', of coorse, if we agree to-night, I think our best plan is to have ourselves called on Sunday. An' I'll tell you what, *avourneen*—be the holy vestments, if I was to be 'called' to fifty on the same Sunday, you're the darlin' I'd marry."

"Phelim, it's time for us to go up to the fire; we're long enough here. I thought you had only three words to say to me."

"Why, if you're tired o' me, Peggy, I don't want you to stop. I wouldn't force myself on the best girl that ever stepped."

"Sure, you have tould me all you want to say, an' there's no use in us stayin' here. You know, Phelim, there's not a girl in the parish ud believe a word that ud come out o' your lips. Sure, there's none o' them but you coorted one time or other. If you could get betther, Phelim, I dunna whether you'd be here to-night at all or not."

"Answer me this, Peggy—what do you think your father ud be willin' to give you? Not that I care a *crona bawn* about it, for I'd marry you wid an inch of candle."

"You know my father's but a poor man, Phelim, an' can give little or nothin'. Them that won't marry me as I am needn't come here to look for a fortune."

"I know that, Peggy, an', be the same a-token, I want no fortune at all wid you but yourself, darlin'. In the manetime, to show you that I could get a fortune—*Dher a lorha heena*, I could have a wife wid a hundher' an' twenty guineas!"

Peggy received this intelligence much in the same manner as Larry and Sheelah had received it. Her mirth was absolutely boisterous for at least ten minutes. Indeed, so loud had it been, that Larry and her father could not help asking—

"*Arrah*, what's the fun, Peggy *achora*?"

"Oh, nothin'," she replied, "but one o' Phelim's bounces."

"Now," said Phelim, "you won't believe me! Be all the books——"

Peggy's mirth prevented his oaths from being heard. In vain he declared, protested, and swore. On this occasion he was compelled to experience the fate peculiar to all liars. Even truth from his lips was looked upon as falsehood.

61

Phelim, on finding that he could neither extort from Peggy an acknowledgment of love, nor make himself credible upon the subject of the large fortune, saw that he had nothing for it now, in order to produce an impression, but the pathetic.

"Well," said he, "you may lave me, Peggy *achora*, if you like; but out o' this I'll not budge, wid a blessin', till I cry my skinful, so I won't. Saize the toe I'll move, now, till I'm sick wid cryin'! Oh, murdher alive, this night! Isn't it a poor case entirely, that the girl I'd suffer myself to be turned inside out for won't say that she cares about a hair o' my head! Oh, thin, but I'm the misfortunate blackguard all out! Och, oh! Peggy *achora*, you'll break my heart! Hand me that shell, *acushla*—for I'm in the height of affliction!"

Peggy could neither withhold it nor reply to him. Her mirth was even more intense now than before; nor, if all were known, was Phelim less affected with secret laughter than Peggy.

"Is it makin' fun o' me you are, you thief—eh? Is it laughin' at my grief you are?" exclaimed Phelim. "Be the tarn o' war, I'll punish you for that."

Peggy attempted to escape; but Phelim succeeded, ere she went, in taking a salutation or two, after which both joined those who sat at the fire, and in a few minutes Sam Appleton entered.

Much serious conversation had already passed in reference to the courtship, which was finally entered into and debated, *pro* and *con*.

"Now, Paddy Donovan, that we're all together, let me tell you one thing—there's not a betther-natur'd boy, nor a stouther, claner young fellow, in the parish than my Phelim. He'll make your daughther as good a husband as ever broke bread!"

"I'm not sayin' aginst that, Larry. He is a good-nathured boy. But I tell you, Larry Toole, my daughther's his fill of a wife any day. An' I'll put this to the back o' that—she's a hard-workin' girl, that ates no idle bread."

"Very right," said Sam Appleton. "Phelim's a hairo, an' she's a beauty. Dang me, but they wor made for one another. Phelim, *abouchal*, why don't you—Oh, I see you are. Why, I was goin' to bid you make up to her."

"Give no *gosther*, Sam," replied Phelim, "but sind round

62

the bottle, an' don't forget to let it come this way. I hardly tasted a dhrop to-night."

"Oh, Phelim!" exclaimed Peggy.

"Whisht!" said Phelim; "there's no use in lettin' the ould fellows be committin' sin. Why, they're hearty[1] as it is, the sinners."

"Come, nabours," said Burn, "I'm the boy that's for close work. How does the match stand? You're both my friends, an' may this be poison to me, but I'll spake like an honest man for the one as well as for the other."

"Well, then," said Donovan, "how is Phelim to support my daughther, Larry? Sure, that's a fair questin', anyway."

"Why, Paddy," replied Larry, "when Phelim gets her, he'll have a patch of his own, as well as another. There's that 'half acre,' and a betther piece o' land isn't in Europe!"

"Well, but what plenishin' are they to have, Larry? A bare half acre's but a poor look-up."

"I'd as soon you'd not make little of it, in the manetime," replied Larry, rather warmly. "As good a couple as ever they wor lived on that half acre; along wid what they earned by hard work otherwise."

"I'm not disparagin' it, Larry; I'd be long sorry. But about the furniture. What are they to begin the world wid?"

"Hut," said Devlin, "go to the sarra wid yees! What ud they want, no more nor other young people like them, to begin the world wid? Are you goin' to make English or Scotch of them, that never marries till they're able to buy a farm an' stock it, the nagers? By the staff in my hand, an Irishman ud lash a dozen o' them, wid all their prudence! Hasn't Phelim an' Peggy health and hands, what most new-married couples in Ireland begins the world wid? Sure, they're not worse nor a thousand others!"

"Success, Antony," said Phelim; "here's your health for that!"

"God be thanked, they have health an' hands," said Donovan. "Still, Antony, I'd like that they'd have some-thin' more."

"Well, then, Paddy, spake up for yourself," observed Larry.

[1] Tipsy.

63

"What will you put to the fore for the *colleen*? Don't take both flesh an' bone!"

"I'll not spake up till I know all that Phelim's to expect," said Donovan. "I don't think he has a right to be axin' anything wid sich a girl as my Peggy."

"Hut, tut, Paddy! She's a good *colleen* enough; but do you think she's above any one that carries the name of O'Toole upon him? Still it's but rasonable for you to wish the girl well settled. My Phelim will have one-half o' my worldly goods, at all evints."

"Name them, Larry, i' you plase."

"Why, he'll have one o' the goats—the grey one, for she's the best o' the two, in throth. He'll have two stools, three hens, an' a toss-up for the cock; the biggest o' the two pots, two good crocks, three good wooden trenchers, an'—hem—he'll have his own—I say, Paddy, are you listenin' to me?—Phelim, do you hear what I'm givin' you, *a veehonee?*—his own bed! An' there's all I can or will do for him. Now do you spake up for Peggy."

"I'm to have my own bedstead too!" said Phelim; "an' bad cess to the stouter one in Europe. It's as good this minute as it was eighteen years agone."

"Paddy Donovan, spake up," said Larry.

"Spake up!" said Paddy contemptuously. "Is it for three crowns' worth I'd spake up? The bedstead, Phelim! *Be dhu husht,* man!"

"Put round the bottle," said Phelim; "we're dhry here."

"Thrue enough, Phelim," said the father. "Paddy, here's towarst you an' yours—nabours, all your healths—young couple! Paddy, give us your hand, man alive! Sure, whether we agree or not, this won't put between us."

"Throth, it won't, Larry—an' I'm thankful to you. Your health, Larry, an' all your healths! Phelim and Peggy, success to yees, whether or not! An' now, in regard o' your civility, I will spake up. My proposal is this—I'll put down guinea for guinea wid you."

Now we must observe, by the way, that this was said under the firm conviction that neither Phelim nor the father had a guinea in their possession.

"I'll do the same, Paddy," said Larry; "but I'll lave it to

the present company if you're not bound to put down the first guinea. Nabours, amn't I right?"

"You are right, Larry," said Burn; "it's but fair that Paddy should put down the first."

"Molly *achora*," said Donovan to the wife, who, by the way, was engaged in preparing the little feast usual on such occasions—"Molly *achora*, give me that ould glove you have in your pocket."

She immediately handed him an old shammy[1] glove, tied up into a hard knot, which he felt some difficulty in unloosing.

"Come, Larry," said he, laying down a guinea-note, "cover that like a man."

"Phelim carries my purse," observed the father; but he had scarcely spoken when the laughter of the company rang loudly through the house. The triumph of Donovan appeared to be complete, for he thought the father's allusion to Phelim tantamount to an evasion.

"Phelim! Phelim carries it! Faix, an' I doubt he finds it a light burdyeen."

Phelim approached in all his glory.

"What am I to do?" he inquired, with a swagger.

"You're to cover that guinea-note wid a guinea, if you can," said Donovan.

"Whether ud you prefar goold or notes?" said Phelim, looking pompously about him; "that's the talk."

This was received with another merry peal of laughter.

"Oh, goold—goold by all manes!" replied Donovan.

"Here goes the goold, my worthy," said Phelim, laying down his guinea with a firm slap upon the table.

Old Donovan seized it, examined it, then sent it round, to satisfy himself that it was a *bonâ fide* guinea.

On finding that it was good he became blank a little; his laugh lost its strength, much of his jollity was instantly neutralised, and his face got at least two inches longer. Larry now had the laugh against him, and the company heartily joined in it.

"Come, Paddy," said Larry, "go an!—ha, ha, ha!"

Paddy fished for half a minute through the glove; and,

[1] Chamois.

after what was apparently a hard chase, brought up another guinea, which he laid down.

"Come, Phelim!" said he, and his eye brightened again with a hope that Phelim would fail.

"Good agin!" said Phelim, thundering down another, which was instantly subjected to a similar scrutiny.

"You'll find it good," said Larry. "I wish we had a sackful o' them. Go an, Paddy. Go an, man; who's afeard?"

"Sowl, I'm done," said Donovan, throwing down the purse with a hearty laugh. "Give me your hand, Larry. Be the goold afore us, I thought to do you. Sure, these two guineas is for my rint, an' we mustn't let them come atween us at all."

"Now," said Larry, "to let you see that my son's not widout something to begin the world wid—Phelim, shell out the rest o' the yallow boys."

"Faix, you ought to dhrink the ould woman's health for this," said Phelim. "Poor ould crathur, many a long day she was saving up these for me. It's my mother I'm speakin' about."

"An' we will, too," said the father: "here's Sheelah's health, nabours !— the best poor man's wife that ever threwn a gown over her shouldher."

This was drunk with all the honours, and the negotiation proceeded.

"Now," said Appleton, "what's to be done? Paddy, say what you'll do for the girl."

"Money's all talk," said Donovan; "I'll give the girl the two-year-old heifer—an' that's worth double what his father has promised Phelim! I'll give her a stone o' flax, a dacent suit o' clo'es, my blessin'—an' there's her fortune."

"Has she neither bed nor beddin'?" inquired Larry.

"Why, don't you say that Phelim's to have his own bed?" observed Donovan. "Sure, one bed 'ill be plenty for them."

"I don't care a damn about fortune," said Phelim, for the first time taking a part in the bargain, "so long as I get the darlin' herself. But I think there ud be no harm in havin' a spare pair o' blankets—an', for that matther, a bed-stead, too—in case a friend came to see a body."

66

"I don't much mind givin' you a brother to the bedstead you have, Phelim," replied Donovan, winking at the company, for he was perfectly aware of the nature of Phelim's bedstead.

"I'll tell you what you must do," said Larry, "otherwise I'll not stand it. Give the *colleen* a chaff bed, blankets, an' all other parts complate, along wid that slip of a pig. If you don't do this, Paddy Donovan, why, we'll finish the whisky, an' part friends—but it's no match."

"I'll never do it, Larry. The bed an' beddin' I'll give; but the pig I'll by no manner o' manes part wid."

"Put round the bottle," said Phelim, "we're gettin' dhry agin—saying nothin' is dhroothy work. Ould man, will you not bother us about fortune!"

"Come, Paddy Donovan," said Devlin, "dang it, let out a little; considher he has ten guineas; an' I give it as my downright maxim an' opinion that he's fairly entitled to the pig."

"You're welcome to give your opinion, Antony, an' I'm welcome not to care a rotten sthraw about it. My daughther's wife enough for him, widout a gown to her back, if he had his ten guineas doubled."

"An' my son," said Larry, "is husband enough for a betther girl nor ever called you father—not makin' little, at the same time, of either you or her."

"Paddy," said Burn, "there's no use in spakin' that way. I agree wid Antony that you ought to throw in the 'slip.'"

"Is it what I have to pay my next gale o' rint wid? No, no! If he won't marry her widout it, she'll get as good that will."

"Saize the 'slip,'" said Phelim, "the darlin' herself here is all the 'slip' I want."

"But I'm not so," said Larry; "the 'slip' must go in, or it's a break-off. Phelim can get girls that has money enough to buy us all out o' root. Did you hear that, Paddy Donovan?"

"I hear it," said Paddy, "but I'll b'lieve as much of it as I like."

Phelim apprehended that, as his father got warm with the liquor, he might, in vindicating the truth of his own assertion, divulge the affair of the old housekeeper.

"Ould man," said he, "have sinse, an' pass that over, if you have any regard for me."

"I'd not be brow-bate into anything," observed Donovan.

"Sowl, you would not," said Phelim. "For my part, Paddy, I'm ready to marry your daughther—(a squeeze to Peggy)—widout a hap'orth at all, barrin' herself. It's the girl I want, an' not the 'slip.'"

"Thin, be the book, you'll get both, Phelim, for your dacency," said Donovan; "but, you see, I wouldn't be bullied into puttin' one foot past the other for the best man that ever stepped on black leather."

"Whisht!" said Appleton, "that's the go! Success, ould heart! Give us your hand, Paddy; here's your good health, an' may you never button an empty pocket!"

"Is all settled?" inquired Molly.

"All but about the weddin' an' the calls," replied her husband. "How are we to do about that, Larry?"

"Why, in the name o' goodness, to save time," he replied, "let them be called on Sunday next, the two Sundays afther, and thin marrid, wid a blessin'."

"I agree wid that entirely," observed Molly. "An' now, Phelim, clear away, you an' Peggy, off o' that chist, till we have our bit o' supper in comfort."

"Phelim," said Larry, "when the supper's done, you must slip over to Roche's for a couple o' bottles more o' whisky. We'll make a night of it."

"There's two bottles in the house," said Donovan; "an', be the saikerment, the first man that talks of bringin' in more till these is dhrunk is ondacent."

This was decisive. In the meantime the chest was turned into a table, the supper laid, and the attack commenced. All was pleasure, fun, and friendship. The reader may be assured that Phelim, during the negotiation, had not mis-spent the time with Peggy. Their conversation, however, was in a tone too low to be heard by those who were them-selves talking loudly.

One thing, however, Phelim understood from his friend Sam Appleton, which was, that some clue had been dis-covered to an outrage in which he (Appleton) had been concerned. Above all other subjects, that was one on which

Phelim was but a poor comforter. He himself found circumspection necessary; and he told Appleton that if ever danger approached him, he had resolved either to enlist, or to go to America, if he could command the money.

"You ought to do that immediately," added Phelim.

"Where's the money?" replied the other.

"I don't know," said Phelim; "but if I was bent on goin', the want of money wouldn't stop me, as long as it could be found in the counthry. We had to do as bad for others, an' it can't be a greater sin to do that much for ourselves."

"I'll think of it," said Appleton. "At any rate, it's in for a penny, in for a pound, wid me."

When supper was over they resumed their drinking, sang songs, and told anecdotes with great glee and hilarity. Phelim and Peggy danced jigs and reels, whilst Appleton sang for them, and the bottle also did its duty.

On separating about two o'clock there was not a sober man among them but Appleton. He declined drinking, and was backed in his abstemiousness by Phelim, who knew that sobriety on the part of Sam would leave himself more liquor. Phelim therefore drank for them both, and that to such excess that Larry, by Appleton's advice, left him at his father's, in consequence of his inability to proceed homewards. It was not, however, without serious trouble that Appleton could get Phelim and the father separated; and when he did, Larry's grief was bitter in the extreme. By much entreaty, joined to some vigorous shoves towards the door, he was prevailed upon to depart without him; but the old man compensated for the son's absence by indulging in the most vociferous sorrow as he went along, about "his Phelim." When he reached home his grief burst out afresh; he slapped the palms of his hands together, and indulged in a continuous howl, that one on hearing it would imagine to be the very echo of misery. When he had fatigued himself he fell asleep on the bed, without having undressed, where he lay until near nine o'clock the next morning. Having got up and breakfasted, he related to his wife, with an aching head, the result of the last night's proceedings. Everything, he assured her, was settled; Phelim and Peggy were to be called the following Sunday, as Phelim, he supposed, had already informed her.

"Where's Phelim?" said the wife; "an' why didn't he come home wid you last night?"

"Where is Phelim! Why, Sheelah woman, sure he did come home wid me last night!"

"*Chrosh orrin*, Larry, no! What could happen him? Why, man, I thought you knew where he was; an' in regard of his bein' abroad so often at night, myself didn't think it sthrange."

Phelim's absence astounded them both, particularly the father, who had altogether forgotten everything that had happened on the preceding night after the period of his intoxication. He proposed to go back to Donovan's to inquire for him, and was about to proceed there when Phelim made his appearance, dressed in his own slender apparel only. His face was three inches longer than usual, and the droop in his eye remarkably conspicuous.

"No fear of him," said the father—"here's himself. *Arrah*, Phelim, what became of you last night? Where wor you?"

Phelim sat down very deliberately and calmly, looked dismally at his mother, and then looked more dismally at his father.

"I suppose you're sick too, Phelim," said the father. "My head's goin' round like a top."

"Ate your breakfast," said his mother; "it's the best thing for you."

"Where wor you last night, Phelim?" inquired the father.

"What are you sayin', ould man?"

"Who wor you wid last night?"

"Do, Phelim," said the mother, "tell us, *aroon!* I hope it wasn't *out* you wor. Tell us, *avourneen!*"

"Ould woman, what are you talkin' about?"

Phelim whistled *Ulican dhu oh*, or the "Song of Sorrow." At length he bounced to his feet, and exclaimed in a loud, rapid voice—

"*Ma chorp an diouol!* ould couple, but I'm robbed of my ten guineas by Sam Appleton!"

"Robbed by Sam Appleton! Heavens above!" exclaimed the father.

"Robbed by Sam Appleton! *Gra machree*, Phelim! no, you aren't!" exclaimed the mother.

70

"*Gra machree* yourself, but I say I am," replied Phelim—"robbed clane of every penny of it!"

Phelim then sat down to breakfast—for he was one of those happy mortals whose appetite is rather sharpened by affliction—and immediately related to his father and mother the necessity which Appleton's connection had imposed on him of leaving the country; adding, that while he was in a state of intoxication he had been stripped of Appleton's clothes; that his own were left beside him; that when he awoke the next morning he found his borrowed suit gone; that on searching for his own he found, to his misery, that the ten guineas had disappeared along with Appleton, who, he understood from his father, had "left the neighbourhood for a while, till the throuble he was in ud pass over."

"But I know where he's gone," said Phelim, "an' may the divil's luck go wid him; an' God's curse on the day I ever had anything to do wid that hell-fire Ribbon business! 'Twas he first brought me into it, the villain; an' now I'd give the townland we're in to be fairly out of it."

"*Hanim an diouol!*" said the father, "is the ten guineas gone? The curse of hell upon him, for a black desaver! Where's the villain, Phelim?"

"He's gone to America," replied the son. "The divil tear the tongue out o' myself, too! I should be puttin' him up to go there, an' to get money, if it was to be had. The villain bit me fairly."

"Well, but how are we to manage?" inquired Larry. "What's to be done?"

"Why," said the other, "to bear it, an' say nothin'. Even if he was in his father's house, the double-faced villain has me so much in his power that I couldn't say a word about it. My curse on the Ribbon business, I say, from my heart out!"

That day was a miserable one to Phelim and the father. The loss of the ten guineas and the feverish sickness produced by their debauch rendered their situation not enviable. Some other small matters, too, in which Phelim was especially concerned, independent of the awkward situation in which he felt himself respecting the three calls on the following day, which was Sunday, added greater weight to his anxiety. He knew not how to manage, especially upon the subject of his

71

habiliments, which certainly were in a very dilapidated state. An Irishman, however, never despairs. If he has not apparel of his own sufficiently decent to wear on his wedding-day, he borrows from a friend. Phelim and his father remembered that there were several neighbours in the village who would oblige him with a suit for the wedding; and as to the other necessary expenses, they did what their countrymen are famous for—they trusted to chance.

"We'll work ourselves out of it some way," said Larry. "Sure, if all fails us, we can sell the goats for the weddin' expenses. It's one comfort that Paddy Donovan must find the dinner; an' all we have to get is the whisky, the marriage-money, an' some other thrifles."

"They say," observed Phelim, "that people have more luck whin they're marrid [1] than whin they're single. I'll have a bout at the marriage, so I will; for worse luck I can't have, if I had half a dozen wives, than I always met wid."

"I'll go down," observed Larry, "to Paddy Donovan's an' send him to the priest's to give in your names to be called to-morrow. Faith, it's well that you won't have to appear, or I dunna how you'd get over it."

"No," said Phelim, "that bill won't pass. You must go to the priest yourself, an' see the curate; if you go near Father O'Hara, it ud knock a plan on the head that I've invinted. I'm in the notion that I'll make the ould woman bleed agin. I'll squeeze as much out of her as 'ill bring me to America, for I'm not overly safe here; or, if all fails, I'll marry her, an' run away wid the money. It ud bring us all acrass."

Larry's interview with the curate was but a short one. He waited on Donovan, however, before he went, who expressed himself satisfied with the arrangement, and looked forward to the marriage as certain. As for Phelim, the idea of being called to three females at the same time was one that tickled his vanity very much. Vanity where the fair sex was concerned had been always his predominant failing. He was not finally determined on marriage with any of them; but

---

[1] This is another absurd opinion peculiar to the Irish, and certainly one of the most pernicious that prevails among them.

he knew that should he even escape the three, the *éclat* resulting from so celebrated a transaction would recommend him to the sex for the remainder of his life. Impressed with this view of the matter, he sauntered about as usual; saw Foodle Flattery's daughter, and understood that her uncle had gone to the priest to have his niece and worthy Phelim called the next day. But besides this hypothesis, Phelim had another, which, after all, was the real one. He hoped that the three applications would prevent the priest from calling him at all.

The priest, who possessed much sarcastic humour, on finding the name of Phelim come in as a candidate for marriage honours with three different women, felt considerably puzzled to know what he could be at. That Phelim might hoax one or two of them was very probable; but that he should have the effrontery to make him the instrument of such an affair, he thought a little too bad.

"Now," said he to his curate, as they talked the matter over that night, "it is quite evident that this scapegrace reckons upon our refusing to call him with any of those females to-morrow. It is also certain that not one of the three to whom he has pledged himself is aware that he is under similar obligations to the other two."

"How do you intend to act, sir?" inquired the curate.

"Why," said Father O'Hara, "certainly to call him to each; it will give the business a turn for which he is not prepared. He will stand exposed, moreover, before the congregation, and that will be some punishment to him."

"I don't know as to the punishment," replied the curate. "If ever a human being was free from shame, Phelim is. The fellow will consider it a joke."

"Very possible," observed his superior; "but I am anxious to punish this old woman. It may prevent her from uniting herself with a fellow who would, on becoming master of her money, immediately abandon her—perhaps proceed to America."

"It will also put the females of the parish on their guard against him," said the innocent curate, who knew not that it would raise him highly in their estimation.

"We will have a scene, at all events," said Father O'Hara;

73

" for I'm resolved to expose him. No blame can be attached to those whom he has duped, excepting only the old woman, whose case will certainly excite a great deal of mirth. That matters not, however; she has earned the ridicule, and let her bear it."

It was not until Sunday morning that the three calls occurred to Phelim in a new light. He forgot that the friends of the offended parties might visit upon his proper carcass the contumely he offered to them. This, however, did not give him much anxiety, for Phelim was never more in his element than when entering upon a row.

The Sunday in question was fine, and the congregation unusually large : one would think that all the inhabitants of the parish of Teernarogarah had been assembled. Most of them certainly were.

The priest, after having gone through the usual ceremonies of the Sabbath worship, excepting those with which he concludes the mass, turned round to the congregation, and thus addressed them :—

"I would not," said he, " upon any other occasion of this kind think it necessary to address you at all; but this is one perfectly unique, and in some degree patriarchal, because, my friends, we are informed that it was allowed in the times of Abraham and his successors to keep more than one wife. This custom is about being revived by a modern, who wants, in rather a barefaced manner, to palm himself upon us as a patriarch. And who do you think, my friends, this Irish patriarch is? Why, no other than bouncing Phelim O'Toole !"

This was received precisely as the priest had anticipated : loud were the shouts of laughter from all parts of the congregation.

"Divil a fear o' Phelim !" they exclaimed. " He wouldn't be himself or he'd kick up a dust some way."

"Blessed Phelim ! Jist like him ! Faith, he couldn't be marrid in the common coorse !"

"*Arrah,* whisht till we hear the name o' the happy crathur that's to be blisthered wid Phelim ! The darlin's in luck, whoever she is, an' has gained a prize in the ' bouncer.' "

"This patriarch," continued the priest, "has made his selection with great judgment and discrimination. In the first place, he has pitched upon a hoary damsel of long standing in the world—one blessed with age and experience. She is qualified to keep Phelim's house well, as soon as it shall be built; but whether she will be able to keep Phelim himself is another consideration. It is not unlikely that Phelim, in imitation of his great prototypes, may prefer living in a tent. But whether she keeps Phelim or the house, one thing is certain, that Phelim will keep her money. Phelim selected this aged woman, we presume, for her judgment; for surely she who has given such convincing proof of discretion must make a useful partner to one who, like Phelim, has that virtue yet to learn. I have no doubt, however, but in a short time he will be as discreet as his teacher."

"Blood alive! Isn't that fine language?"

"You may say that! Begad, it's himself can discoorse! What's the Protestants to that?"

"The next upon the list is one who, though a poor man's daughter, will certainly *bring property* to Phelim. There is also an aptness in this selection which does credit to the 'Patriarch.' Phelim is a great dancer, an accomplishment of which we do not read that the patriarchs themselves were possessed; although we certainly do read that a light heel was of a little service to Jacob. Well, Phelim carries a light heel, and the second female of his choice on this list carries a 'light hand';[1] it is therefore but natural to suppose that, if ever they are driven to extremities, they will make light of many things which other people would consider of weighty moment. Whether Phelim and she may long remain stationary in this country is a problem more likely to be solved at the county assizes than here. It is not improbable that his Majesty may recommend the patriarch and one of his wives to try the benefit of a voyage to New South Wales, he himself graciously vouchsafing to bear their expenses."

"Divil a lie in that, anyhow! If ever any one crossed the wather, Phelim will. Can't his reverence be funny when he plases?"

---

[1] Intimating theft.

75

"Many a time it was prophecized for him; an' his reverence knows best."

"Begad, Phelim's gettin' over the coals. But sure it's all the way the father an' mother reared him."

"Tundher-an'-turf, is he goin' to be called to a pair o' them?"

"Faix, so it seems."

"Oh, the divil's clip! Is he mad? But let us hear it out."

"The third damsel is by no means so well adapted for Phelim as either of the other two. What she could have seen in him is another problem much more difficult than the one I have mentioned. I would advise her to reconsider the subject, and let Phelim have the full benefit of the attention she may bestow upon it. If she finds the patriarch possessed of but one virtue, except necessity, I will admit that it is pretty certain that she will soon discover the longitude, and that has puzzled the most learned men of the world. If she marries this patriarch, I think the angels who may visit him will come in shape of policemen; and that Phelim, so long as he can find a cudgel, will give them anything but a patriarchal reception is another thing of which we may rest pretty certain.

"I now publish the banns of matrimony between Phelim O'Toole of Teernarogarah and Bridget Doran of Dernascobe. If any person knows of any impediment why these two should not be joined in wedlock, they are bound to declare it.

"This Bridget Doran, my friends, is no other than my old housekeeper; but when, where, or how Phelim could have won upon her juvenile affections is one of those mysteries which is never to be explained. I dare say the match was brought about by despair on her side, and necessity on his. She despaired of getting a husband, and he had a necessity for the money. In point of age I admit she would make a very fit wife for any patriarch."

Language could not describe the effect which this disclosure produced upon the congregation. The fancy of every one present was tickled at the idea of a union between Phelim and the old woman. It was followed by roars of laughter, which lasted several minutes.

"Oh, thin, the curse o' the crows upon him, was he only

76

able to butther up the ould woman! Oh, *Ghe dhiven!* that
flogs. Why, it's a wondher he didn't stale the ould slip, an'
make a runaway match of it!—ha, ha, ha! *Musha,* bad scran
to her, but she had young notions of her own! A purty bird
she picked up in Phelim!—ha, ha, ha!"

"I also publish the banns of matrimony between Phelim
O'Toole of Teernarogarah and Sally Flattery of the same
place. If any of you know of any impediment why they
should not be joined in wedlock, you are bound to declare it."

The mirth rose again loud and general. Foodle Flattery,
whose character was so well known, appeared so proper a
father-in-law for Phelim that his selection in this instance
delighted them highly.

"Betther an' betther, Phelim! More power to you!
You're fixed at last. Foodle Flattery's daughter—a known
thief! Well, what harm? Phelim himself has pitch on his
fingers—or had, anyhow, when he was growin' up—for many
a thing stuck to them. Oh, bedad, now we know what his
reverence was at when he talked about the 'sizes, bad luck
to them! Betune her an' the ould woman, Phelim ud be in
Paradise! Foodle Flattery's daughter! Begad, she'll 'bring
him property,' sure enough, as his reverence says."

"I also publish the banns of matrimony between Phelim
O'Toole—whom we must in future call the 'Patriarch'—of
Teernarogarah, and Peggy Donovan of the same place. If
any of you know any impediment in the way of their marriage,
you are bound to declare it."

"Bravo! Phelim, *acushla.* 'Tis you that's the blessed
youth. Tundher-an'-whisky, did ever anybody hear of such
desate? To do three o' them! Be sure the bouncer has
some schame in this. Well, one would suppose Paddy Donovan an' his daughter had more sinse nor to think of sich a
runagate as bouncin' Phelim."

"No, but the pathriark! Sure, his reverence sez that
we mustn't call him anything agin but the pathriark! Oh,
begorra, that's the name!—ha, ha, ha!"

When the mirth of the congregation had subsided, and
their comments ended, the priest concluded in the following
words:—

"Now, my friends, here is such a piece of profligacy as I

have never, in the whole course of my pastoral duties, witnessed. It is the act of Phelim O'Toole, be it known, who did not scruple to engage himself for marriage to three females —that is, to two girls and an old woman—and who, in addition, had the effrontery to send me his name and theirs, to be given out all on the same Sunday; thus making me an instrument in his hands to hoax those who trusted in his word. That he can marry but one of them is quite clear; but that he would not scruple to marry the three, and three more to complete the half-dozen, is a fact which no one who knows him will doubt. For my part, I know not how this business may terminate. Of a truth he has contrived to leave the claims of the three females in a state of excellent confusion. Whether it raise or lessen him in their opinion, I cannot pretend to determine. I am sorry for Donovan's daughter, for I know not what greater calamity could befall any honest family than a matrimonial union with Phelim O'Toole. I trust that this day's proceedings will operate as a caution to the females of the parish against such an unscrupulous reprobate. It is for this purpose only that I publish the names given in to me. His character was pretty well known before; it is now established; and having established it, I dismiss the subject altogether."

Phelim's fame was now nearly at its height. Never before had such a case been known; yet the people somehow were not so much astonished as might be supposed; on the contrary, had Phelim's courtship gone off like that of another man they would have felt more surprised. We need scarcely say that the "giving out" or "calling" of Phelim and the three damsels was spread over the whole parish before the close of that Sunday. Every one had it—man, woman, and child. It was told, repeated, and improved as it went along. New circumstances were added, fresh points made out, and other *dramatis personæ* brought in—all with great felicity, and quite suitable to Phelim's character.

Strongly contrasted with the amusement of the parishioners in general was the indignation felt by the three damsels and their friends. The old housekeeper was perfectly furious; so much so, indeed, that the priest gave some dark hints at the necessity of sending for a strait waistcoat. Her fellow-servants took the liberty of breaking some strong jests upon her, in return for which she took the liberty of breaking two strong churn-staves upon them. Being a remarkably strong woman for her years, she put forth her strength to such purpose that few of them went to bed without sore bones. The priest was seriously annoyed at it, for he found that his house was a scene of battle during the remainder of the day.

Sally Flattery's uncle, in the absence of her father, indignantly espoused the cause of his niece. He and Donovan each went among their friends to excite in them a proper resentment, and to form a faction for the purpose of chastising Phelim. Their chagrin was bitter on finding that their most wrathful representations of the insult sustained by their families were received with no other spirit than one of the most extravagant mirth. In vain did they rage, and fume, and swear; they could get no one to take a serious view of it. Phelim O'Toole was the author of all, and from him it was precisely what they had expected.

Phelim himself, and the father, on hearing of the occurrence after mass, were as merry as any other two in the parish. At first the father was disposed to lose his temper; but on Phelim telling him he would hear no *gosther* on the subject, he thought proper to take it in good-humour. About this time they had not more than a week's provision in the house, and only three shillings of capital. The joke of the three calls was too good a one to pass off as an ordinary affair —they had three shillings, and although it was their last, neither of them could permit the matter to escape as a dry joke. They accordingly repaired to the little public-house of the village, where they laughed at the world, got drunk, hugged each other, despised all mankind, and staggered home, ragged and merry, poor and hearty, their arms about each other's necks, perfect models of filial duty and paternal affection.

The reader is aware that the history of Phelim's abrupt engagement with the housekeeper was conveyed by Fool Art to Sally Flattery. Her thievish character rendered marriage as hopeless to her as length of days did to Bridget Doran. No one knew the plan she had laid for Phelim, but this fool; and in order to secure his silence she had promised him a shirt on the Monday after the first call. Now Art, as was evident by his endless habit of shrugging, felt the necessity of a shirt very strongly.

About ten o'clock on Monday he presented himself to Sally, and claimed his recompense.

"Art," said Sally, "the shirt I intended for you is upon Squire Nugent's hedge beside their garden. You know the family's goin' up to Dublin on Thursday, Art, an' they're gettin' their washin' done in time to be off. Go down, but don't let any one see you; take the third shirt on the row, an' bring it up to me till I smooth it for you."

Art sallied down to the hedge on which the linen had been put out to dry, and having reconnoitred the premises, shrugged himself, and cast a longing eye on the third shirt. With that knavish penetration, however, peculiar to such persons, he began to reflect that Sally might have some other object in view besides his accommodation. He determined therefore to proceed upon new principles—sufficiently safe, he thought, to protect him from the consequences of theft.

"Good-morrow, Bush," said Art, addressing that on which the third shirt was spread. "Isn't it a burnin' shame an' a sin for you," he continued, "to have sich a fine white shirt an you, an' me widout a stitch to my back. Will you swap?"

Having waited until the bush had due time to reply—

"Sorra fairer," he observed; "silence gives consint."

In less than two minutes he stripped, put on one of the Squire's best shirts, and spread out his own dusky fragment in its place.

"It's a good thing," said Art, "to have a clear conscience; a fair exchange is no robbery."

Now, it so happened that the Squire himself, who was a humourist, and also a justice of the peace, saw Art putting his morality in practice at the hedge. He immediately walked out with an intention of playing off a trick upon the fool for his dishonesty; and he felt the greater inclination to do this in consequence of an opinion long current, that Art, though he had outwitted several, had never been outwitted himself.

Art had been always a welcome guest in the Squire's kitchen, and never passed the "Big House," as an Irish country gentleman's residence is termed, without calling. On this occasion, however, he was too cunning to go near it—a fact which the Squire observed. By taking a short cut across one of his own fields he got before Art, and turning the angle of a hedge, met him trotting along at his usual pace.

"Well, Art, where now?"

"To the crass roads, your honour."

"Art, is not this a fine place of mine? Look at these groves, and the lawn, and the river there, and the mountains behind all. Is it not equal to Sir William R——'s?"[1] (Sir William was Art's favourite patron.)

"Sir William, your honour, has all this at his place."

"But I think my views are finer."

"They're fine enough," replied Art; "but where's the lake before the door?"

The Squire said no more about his prospects.

"Art," he continued, "would you carry a letter for me to M——?"

"I'll be wantin' somethin' to dhrink on the way," said Art.

"You shall get something to eat and drink before you go," said the Squire, "and half-a-crown for your trouble."

"Augh," exclaimed Art, "be dodda, sir, you're nosed like Sir William, and chinned like Captain Taylor." This was always Art's compliment when pleased.

The Squire brought him up to the house, ordered him refreshment, and while Art partook of it, wrote a letter or mittimus to the county gaoler, authorising him to detain the bearer in prison until he should hear further from him.

Art, having received the half-crown and the letter, appeared delighted; but on hearing the name of the person to whom it was addressed, he smelt a trick. He promised faithfully, however, to deliver it, and betrayed no symptoms whatever of suspicion. After getting some distance from

---

[1] A local landlord named Sir W. Richardson, referred to in Carleton's incomplete "Autobiography," recently published, with a continuation by the present writer.—ED.

the big house, he set his wits to work, and ran over in his mind the names of those who had been most in the habit of annoying him. At the head of this list stood Phelim O'Toole, and on Phelim's head did he resolve to transfer the revenge which the Squire, he had no doubt, intended to take on himself.

With considerable speed he made his way to Larry O'Toole's, where such a scene presented itself as made him for a moment forget the immediate purport of his visit.

Opposite Phelim, dressed out in her best finery, stood the housekeeper, zealously insisting on either money or marriage. On one side of him stood old Donovan and his daughter, whom he had forced to come, in the character of a witness, to support his charges against the gay deceiver. On the other were ranged Sally Flattery in tears, and her uncle in wrath, each ready to pounce upon Phelim.

Phelim stood the very emblem of patience and good-humour. When one of them attacked him he winked at the other two; when either of the other two came on he winked still at those who took breath. Sometimes he trod on his father's toe, lest the old fellow might lose the joke, and not unfrequently proposed their going to a public-house, and composing their differences over a bottle, if any of them would pay the expenses.

"What do you mane to do?" said the housekeeper—"but it's asy known I'm an unprotected woman, or I wouldn't be thrated as I am. If I had relations livin' or near me, we'd pay you on the bones for bringin' me to shame and scandal as you have done."

"Upon my *sannies*, Mrs. Doran, I feel for your situation, so I do," said Phelim. "You've outlived all your friends, an' if it was in my power to bring any o' them back to you I'd do it."

"Oh, you desaver, is that the feelin' you have for me, when I thought you'd be a guard an' projection to me? You know I have the money, you sconce, an' how comfortable it ud keep us, if you'd only see what's good for you. You blarneyed an' palavered me, you villain, till you got my infections, an' thin you tuck the colic as an

82

excuse to lave me in a state of dissolution an' disparagement. You promised to marry me, an' you had no notion of it."

"You're not the only one he has disgraced, Mrs. Doran," said Donovan. "A purty way he came down, himself an' his father, undher pretence of coortin' my daughter. He should lay down his ten guineas, too, to show us what he had to begin the world wid, the villain!—an' him had no notion of it aither."

"An' he should send this girl to make me go to the priest to have him and her called, the reprobate!" said Nick Flattery—"an' him had no notion of it aither."

"Sure, he sent us all there!" exclaimed Donovan.

"He did," said the old woman.

"Not a doubt of it," observed Flattery.

"Ten guineas!" said the housekeeper. "An' so you brought my ten guineas in your pocket to coort another girl! Aren't you a right profligate?"

"Yes," said Donovan, "aren't you a right profligate?"

"Answer the dacent people," said Flattery—"aren't you a right profligate?"

"Take the world asy, all of yees," replied Phelim. "Mrs. Doran, there was three of you called, sure enough; but, be the vestments, I intinded—Do you hear me, Mrs. Doran? Now have rason—I say, do you hear me? Be the vestments, I intinded to marry only one of you; an' that I'll do still, except I'm vexed—(a wink at the old woman). Yet you're all flyin' at me, as if I had three heads upon me."

"Maybe the poor boy's not so much to blame," said Mrs. Doran. "There's hussies in this world," and here she threw an angry eye upon the other two, "that ud give a man no pace till he'd promised to marry them."

"Why did he promise to them that didn't want him, thin?" exclaimed Donovan. "I'm not angry that he didn't marry my daughther—for I wouldn't give her to him now—but I am at the slight he put an her."

"Paddy Donovan, did you hear what I said jist now?" replied Phelim. "I wish to Jamini some people ud have sinse! Be them five crasses, I know thim I intinded to marry, as well as I do where I'm standin'. That's plain talk,

Paddy. I'm sure the world's not past yet, I hope"—(a wink at Paddy Donovan).

" An' wasn't he a big rascal to make little of my brother's daughther as he did ? " said Flattery ; " but he'll rub his heels together for the same act."

" Nick Flatthery, do you think I could marry three wives ? Be that horseshoe over the door, Sally Flatthery, you didn't thrate me dacent. She did not, Nick; an' you ought to know that it was wrong of her to come here to-day."

" Well, but what do you intind to do, Phelim, *avourn*—— you profligate ? " said the half-angry, half-pacified house-keeper, who, being the veteran, always led on the charge.

" Why, I intind to marry one of you," said Phelim. " I say, Mrs. Doran, do you see thim ten fingers acrass—be thim five crasses, I'll do what I said, if nothing happens to put it aside."

" Then be an honest man," said Flattery, " an' tell us which o' them you will marry."

" Nick, don't you know I always regarded your family ? If I didn't, that I may never do an ill turn ! Now ! But some people can't see anything. *Arrah*, tundher-an'-whisky, man, would you expect me to tell out, before all that's here, who I'll marry—to be hurtin' the feelins of the rest. Faith, I'll never do a shabby thing."

" What rekimpinse will you make my daughther for bringin' down her name afore the whole parish, along wid them she oughtn't to be named in the one day wid ? " said Donovan.

" An' who is that, Paddy Donovan ? " said the housekeeper, with a face of flame.

" None of your broad hints, Paddy," said Nick. " If it's a collusion to Sally Flattery you mane, take care I don't make you ate your words."

" Paddy," exclaimed Phelim, " you oughtn't to be hurtin' their feelins ! "—(a friendly wink to Paddy).

" If you mane me," said the housekeeper, " by the crook on the fire, I'd lave you a mark."

" I mane you for one, thin, since you provoke me," replied Donovan.

" For one is it ? " said Nick; " an' who's the other, i' you plase ? "

84

"Your brother's daughther," he replied. "Do you think I'd even[1] my daughther to a thief?"

"Begorra," observed Phelim, "that's too provokin', an' what I wouldn't bear. Will yees keep the pace, I say, till I spake a word to Mrs. Doran? Mrs. Doran, can I have a word or two wid you outside the house?"

"To be sure you can," she replied; "I'd give you fair play if the *diouol* was in you."

Phelim accordingly brought her out, and thus accosted her:

"Now, Mrs. Doran, you think I thrated you ondacent; but do you see that book?" said he, producing a book of ballads, on which he had sworn many a similar oath before. "Be the contints o' that book, as sure as you're beside me, it's you I intind to marry! These other two—the curse o' the crows upon them! I wish we could get them from about the place—is both dyin' for love o' me, an' I surely did promise to get myself called to them. They wanted it to be a promise of marriage; but, says I, 'Sure, if we're called together it's the same, for whin it comes to that, all's right' —an' so I tould both o' them, unknownst to one another. *Arrah*, be my sowl, you'd make two like them, so you would; an' if you hadn't a penny, I'd marry you afore aither o' them to-morrow. Now, there's the whole sacret, an' don't be onaisy about it. Tell Father O'Hara how it is, whin you go home, an' that he must call the three o' you to me agin, on next Sunday, and the Sunday afther, plase goodness; jist that I may keep my promise to them. You know I couldn't have luck or grace if I marrid you wid the sin of two broken promises on me."

"My goodness, Phelim, but you tuck a burdyeen off o' me! Faix, you'll see how happy we'll be."

"To be sure we will! But I'm tould you're sometimes crass, Mrs. Doran. Now, you must promise to be kind an' lovin' to the childher, or, be the vestment, I'll break off the match yet."

"Och, an' why wouldn't I, Phelim, *acushla*? Sure, that's but rason."

"Well, take this book an' swear it: Begorra, your word

[1] Compare.

85

won't do, for it's a thing my mind's made up on. It's I that'll be fond o' the childher."

"An' how am I to swear it, Phelim? for I never tuck an oath myself yet."

"Take the book in your hand, shut one eye, and say the words afther me. Be the contints o' this book—"

"Be the contints o' this book—"

"I'll be kind, an' motherly, an' boistherous—"

"I'll be kind, an' motherly, an' boistherous—"

"To my own childher—"

"To my own childher—"

"An' never bate or abuse thim—"

"An' never bate or abuse thim—"

"Barrin' whin they desarve it."

"Barrin' whin they desarve it."

"An' this I swear—"

"An' this I swear—"

"In the presence of St. Phelim."

"In the presence of St. Phelim."

"Amin!"

"Amin!"

"Now, Mrs. Doran, *acushla*, if you could jist know how aisy my conscience is about the childher, poor crathurs, you'd be in mighty fine spirits. There won't be sich a lovin' husband, begad, in Europe. It's I that'll coax you, an' butther you up like a new pair o' brogues; but, begad, you must be sweeter than liquorice or sugar-candy to me. Won't you, darlin'?"

"Be the crass, Phelim darlin', jewel, I'll be as kind a wife as ever breathed! *Arrah*, Phelim, won't you come down to-morrow evenin'? There'll be no one at home but myself, an'—ha, ha, ha!—Oh, you coaxin' rogue! I see you laughin'! Will you come, darlin'?"

"Surely. But death alive! I was near forgettin'—sure, bad luck to the penny o' the ten guineas but I paid away."

"Paid away! Is it my ten guineas?"

"Your ten guineas, darlin'; an' right well I managed it. Didn't I secure Pat Hanratty's farm by it? Sam Appleton's uncle had it as good as taken; so, begad, I came down wid the ten guineas, by way of airles, an' now we have it. I knew you'd be plased to hear it, an' that you'd be proud to give me ten more for clo'es an' the weddin' expenses. Isn't that good news, *avourneen?*—eh, you duck o' diamonds? Faith, let Phelim alone! An' another thing—I must call you Bridget for the future; it's sweeter an' more lovin'."

"Phelim, I wish you had consulted wid me afore you done it; but it can't be helped. Come down to-morrow evenin', an' we'll see what's to be done."

"The grace o' heaven upon you, but you are the winnin'est woman alive this day! Now take my advice, an' go home widout comin' in. I'm wantin' to get this other pair off o' my hands as well as I can; an' our best way is to do all widout noise. Isn't it, darlin'?"

"It is, Phelim, jewel; an' I'll go."

"Faith, Bridget, you've dealt in thracle afore now, you're so sweet. Now, *acushla,* farewell; an' take care of yourself till to-morrow evenin'!"

Phelim, on re-entering his father's cabin, found Larry and Peggy Donovan placed between her father and Flattery, each struggling to keep them asunder. Phelim at first had been anxious to set them by the ears, but his interview with the old woman changed his plan of operations altogether. With some difficulty he succeeded in repressing their tendency to single combat, which having effected, he brought out Flattery and his niece, both of whom he thus addressed—

"Be the vestment, Sally, only that my regard an' love for you is uncommon, I'd break off the affair altogether, so I would."

"An' why would you do so, Phelim O'Toole?" inquired the uncle.

"Bekase," replied Phelim, "you came here an' made a show of me when I wished to have no *brieuliagh* at all, at all. In regard of Peggy Donovan, I never spoke a word to the girl about marriage since I was christened. Saize the syllable! My father brought me down there to *gosther* a while the other night, an' Paddy sent away for whisky. An' the curse o' Cromwell on myself! I should get tossicated. So while I was half-says over, the two ould rips set to makin' the match —planned to have us called—an' me knew nothin' about it, good, bad, or indifferent. That's the thruth, be the sky above us!"

"An' what have you to say about the housekeeper, Phelim?"

"Why, I don't know yet who done me there. I was about takin' a farm, an' my father borrid ten guineas from her. Somebody heard it—I suspect Sam Appleton—an' gave in our names to the priest to be called, makin' a good joke of it. All sorts o' luck to them, barrin' good luck, that did it; but they put me in a purty state! But never heed! I'll find them out yet. Now go home, both o' you, an' I'll slip down in half an hour, wid a bottle o' whisky in my pocket. We'll talk over what's to be done. Sure, Sally here knows it's my own intherest to marry her, and no one else."

"If my father thought you would, Phelim, he'd not stag, even if he was to crass the wather!"

"Go home, Sally darlin', till I get this mad Donovan an' his daughther away. Be all that's beautiful, I'll be apt to give him a taste o' my *shillelagh* if he doesn't behave himself! Half an hour I'll be down in—wid the bottle; an' don't you go, Nick, till you see me."

"Phelim," said the uncle, "you know how the case is: you must aither marry the girl, or take a long voyage, *abouchal*. We'll have no bouncin' or palaver."

"Bedad, Nick, I've great patience wid you," said Phelim, smiling—"go off, I say, both of you."

They then proceeded homewards, and Phelim returned to appease the anger of Donovan, as he had that of the others. Fresh fiction was again drawn forth, every word of which the worthy father corroborated. They promised to go down that night and drink another bottle together; a promise which they knew by the state of their finances it was impossible to fulfil. The prospect of the "booze," however, tranquillised Donovan, who in his heart relished a glass of liquor as well as either Phelim or the father. Shaking of hands and professions of friendship were again beginning to multiply with great rapidity, when Peggy thought proper to make a few observations on the merits of her admirer.

"In regard to me," she observed, "you may save yourselves the throuble o' comin'. I wouldn't marry Phelim, afther what the priest said yistherday, if he had the riches o' the townland we're spakin' in. I never cared for him, nor liked him; an' it was only to plase my father an' mother that I consinted to be called to him at all. I'll never join myself to the likes of him. If I do, may I be a corpse the next minute!"

Having thus expressed herself, she left her father, Phelim, and Larry to digest her sentiments, and immediately went home.

Donovan, who was outrageous at this contempt of his authority, got his hat, with the intention of compelling her to return and retract in their presence what she had said; but the daughter, being the more light-footed of the two, reached home before he could overtake her; where, backed by her mother, she maintained her resolution, and succeeded, ere long, in bringing the father over to her opinion.

During this whole scene in Larry's, Fool Art sat in that wild abstraction which characterises the unhappy class to which he belonged. He muttered to himself, laughed—or rather chuckled—shrugged his shoulders, and appeared to be as unconscious of what had taken place as an automaton. When the coast was clear he rose up, and plucking Phelim's skirt, beckoned him towards the door.

"Phelim," said he, when they had got out, "would you like to earn a crown?"

"Tell me how, Art," said Phelim.

"A letther from the Square to the gaoler of M—— gaol. If you bring back an answer, you'll get a crown, your dinner, an' a quart o' sthrong beer."

"But why don't you bring it yourself, Art?"

"Why, I'm afeard. Sure, they'd keep me in gaol, I'm tould, if they'd catch me in it—aha! Bedad, I won't go near them; sure, they'd hang me for shootin' Bonypart—aha!"

"Must the answer be brought back to-day, Art?"

"Oh, it wouldn't do to-morrow at all. Be dodda, no! Five shillins, your dinner, an' a quart o' sthrong beer!— aha! But you must give me a shillin' or two to buy a sword, for the Square's goin' to make me a captain; thin I'll be grand, an' I'll make you a sargint."

This seemed a windfall to Phelim. The unpleasant dilemma in which Sally Flattery had placed him by the fabricated account of her father's imprisonment made him extremely anxious to see Foodle himself, and to ascertain the precise outrage for which he had been secured. Here, then, was an opportunity of an interview with him, and of earning five shillings, a good dinner, and a quart of strong beer, as already specified.

"Art," said he, "give me the letther, an' I'm the boy that'll soon do the job. Long life to you, Art! Be the contints o' the book, Art, I'll never pelt you or vex you agin, my worthy; an' I'll always call you captain!"

Phelim immediately commenced his journey to M——, which was only five miles distant, and in a very short time reached the gaol, saw the gaoler, and presented his letter.

The latter, on perusing it, surveyed him with the scrutiny of a man whose eye was practised in scanning offenders.

Phelim, whilst the gaoler examined him, surveyed the strong and massy bolts with which every door and hatchway was secured. Their appearance produced rather an uncomfortable sensation in him; so much so, that when the gaoler asked him his name he thought it more prudent, in consequence of a touch of conscience he had, to personate Art for the present, inasmuch as he felt it impossible to assume any name more safe than that of an idiot.

"My name is Art Maguire," said he, in reply to the gaoler. "I'm messenger to Square S——; the one he had was discharged on Friday last. I expect soon to be made groom, too."

"Come this way," said the gaoler, "and you shall have an answer."

He brought Phelim into the prison-yard, where he remained for about twenty minutes, labouring under impressions which he felt becoming gradually more unpleasant. His anxiety was not lessened on perceiving twenty or thirty culprits, under the management of the turnkeys, enter the yard, where they were drawn up in a line, like a file of soldiers.

"What's your name?" said one of the turnkeys.

"Art Maguire," replied Phelim.

"Stand here," said the other, shoving him amongst the prisoners. "Keep your head up, you villain, an' don't be ashamed to look your friends in the face. It won't be hard o identify you, at any rate, you scoundrel. A glimpse of that phiz, even by starlight, would do you, you dog. Jack, tell Mr. S—— to bring in the gintlemen—they're all ready."

Phelim's dismay on finding himself under drill with such a villainous crew was indescribable. He attempted to parley with the turnkey, but was near feeling the weight of his heavy keys for daring to approach a man placed in authority.

While thus chewing the cud of sweet and bitter fancy, three gentlemen, accompanied by the gaoler, entered the yard, and walked backward and forward in front of the prisoners, whose faces and persons they examined with great care. For a considerable time they could not recognise any of them ; but just as they were about to give up the scrutiny, one of the gentlemen approached Phelim, and looking narrowly into his countenance, exclaimed—

" Here, gaoler, this man I identify. I cannot be mistaken in his face ; the rough visage and drooping eye of that fellow put all doubt as to his identity out of question. What's his name ? "

" He gives his name, sir, as Arthur Maguire."

" Arthur what, sir ? " said another of the turnkeys, looking earnestly at Phelim. " Why, sir, this is the fellow that swore the *alibis* for the Kellys—ay, an' for the Delanys, an' for the O'Briens. His name is Phelim O'Toole ; an' a purty boy he is, by all report."

Phelim, though his heart sank within him, attempted to banter them out of their bad opinion of him ; but there was something peculiarly dismal and melancholy in his mirth.

" Why, gintlemen — ha, ha ! — begorra, I'd take it as a convanience—I mane as a favour—if you'd believe me that there's a small taste of mistake here. I was sent by Square S—— wid a letter to Mr. S——t, an' he gave me fifty ordhers to bring him back an' answer this day. As for Phelim O'Toole, if you mane the rascal that swears the *alibis*, faith, I can't deny but I'm as like him, the villain, as one egg is to another. Bad luck to his ' dhroop,' anyhow ; little I thought that it would ever bring me into throuble—ha, ha, ha ! Mr. S——t, what answer have you for the Square, sir ? Bedad, I'm afeard I'll be late."

" That letter, Master Maguire, or Toole, or whatever your

name is, authorises me to detain you as a prisoner until I hear further from Mr. S——."

" I identify him distinctly," said the gentleman once more. " I neither doubt nor waver on the subject; so you will do right to detain him. I shall lodge informations against him immediately."

" Sir," said Phelim to the gaoler, "the Square couldn't mane me at all, in regard that it was another person he gave the letter to, for to bring to you; the other person gave it to me. I can make my oath of that. Begorra, you're playin' your thricks upon sthrangers now, I suppose."

" Why, you lying rascal," said the gaoler, "have you not a few minutes ago asserted to the contrary? Did you not tell me that your name was Arthur, or Art Maguire? that you are Mr. S——'s messenger, and expect to be made his groom? And now you deny all this."

" He's Phelim O'Toole," said the turnkey, " I'll swear to him; but if you wait for a minute I'll soon prove it."

He immediately retired to the cell of a convict whom he knew to be from the townland of Teernarogarah, and ordering its inmate to look through the bars of his window, which commanded the yard, he asked him if there was any one among them whom he knew.

The fellow in a few minutes replied, " Whethen, divil a one, barrin' bouncin' Phelim O'Toole."

The turnkey brought him down to the yard, where he immediately recognised Phelim as an old friend, shook hands with him, and addressed him by his name.

" Bad luck to you," said Phelim, in Irish, " is this a place to welcome your friends to ? "

" There is some mystery here," said the gaoler. " I suppose the fact is that this fellow returned a wrong name to Mr. S——, and that accounts for the name of Arthur Maguire being in the letter."

All Phelim's attempts to extricate himself were useless. He gave them the proper version of the letter affair with Fool Art, but without making the slightest impression : the gaoler desired him to be locked up.

" Divil fire you all, you villains ! " exclaimed Phelim; " is it goin' to put me in crib yees are for no rason in life?

Doesn't the whole parish know that I was never off o' my bed for the last three months, wid a complaint I had, antil widin two or three days agone!"

"There are two excellent motives for putting you in crib," said the gaoler; "but if you can prove that you have been confined to your bed so long as you say, why, it will be all the better for yourself. Go with the turnkey."

"No; tarenation to the fut I'll go," said Phelim, "till I'm carrid."

"Doesn't the gintleman identify you, you villain," replied one of the turnkeys; "an' isn't the Square's letther in your favour?"

"Villain is id!" exclaimed Phelim. "An' from a hangman's cousin, too, we're to bear this!—eh? Take that, anyhow, an' maybe you'll get more when you don't expect it. Whoo! Success, Phelim! There's blood in you still, *abouchal!*"

He accompanied the words by a spring of triumph from the ground, and surveyed the already senseless turnkey with exultation. In a moment, however, he was secured for the purpose of being put into strong irons.

"To the devil's warmin'-pan wid ye all," he continued; "you may do your worst. I defy yees. Ha! be the heavens above me, you'll suffer for this, my fine gintleman. What can yees do but hang or thransport me, you villains? I tell yees, if a man's sowl had a crust of sin on it a foot thick, the best way to get it off ud be jist to shoot a dozen like you. Sin! Oh, the divil saize the sin at all in it. But wait! Did yees ever hear of a man they call Dan O'Connell? Be my sowl, he'll make yees rub your heels together, for keepin' an innocent boy in gaol, that there's no law or no warrant out for. This is the way we're thrated by thim that's ridin' rough shod over us. But have a taste o' patience, ye scoundrels! It won't last, I can tell yees. Our day will soon come, an' then I'd recommend yees to thravel for your health. Hell saize the day's pace or happiness ever will be seen in the country till laws, an' judges, an' juries, an' gaols, an' gaolers, an' turnkeys, an' hangmen is all swep' out of it. Saize the day! An' along wid them goes the parsons an' procthors, tithes an' taxes, all to the divil together. That

93

day's not far off, ye villains. An' now I tell yees, that if a hair o' my head's touched—ay, if I was hanged to-morrow— I'd lave them behind me that ud put a bullet, wid the help an' blessin' o' God, through any one that'll injure me! So lay that to your conscience, an' do your best. Be the crass, O'Connell 'ill make you look nine ways at wanst for this! He's the boy can put the pin in your noses! He's the boy can make yees thrimble, one an' all o' yees—like a dog in a wet sack! An', wid the blessin' o' God, he'll help us to put our feet on your necks afore long!"

"That's a prudent speech," observed the gaoler; "it will serve you very much."

Phelim consigned him to a very warm settlement in reply.

"Come away, Phelim," said the turnkey, "follow me; you are goin' to be put where you'll have an opportunity of sayin' your prayers."

He then ushered Phelim to a cell, where the reader may easily imagine what he felt. His patriotism rose to a high pitch; he deplored the wrongs of his country bitterly, and was clearly convinced that until gaols, judges, and assizes, together with a long train of similar grievances, were utterly abolished, Ireland could never be right, nor persecuted "boys" like himself at full liberty to burn or murder the enemies of their country with impunity. Notwithstanding these heroic sentiments, an indifferent round oath more than once escaped him against Ribbonism in whole and in part. He cursed the system, and the day and the hour on which he was inveigled into it. He cursed those who had initiated him; nor did his father and mother escape for their neglect of his habits, his morals, and his education. This occurred when he had time for reflection.

The next day Fool Art went to Larry's, where he understood that Phelim was on the missing list. This justified his suspicions of the Squire; but by no means lessened his bitterness against him for the prank he had intended to play upon him. With great simplicity he presented himself at the big house, and met its owner on the lawn, accompanied by two other gentlemen. The magistrate was somewhat surprised on seeing Art at large, when he imagined him to be under the gaoler's lock and key.

"Well, Art," said he, concealing his amazement, "did you deliver my letter?"

"It went safe, your honour," replied Art.

"Did you yourself give it into his hands, as I ordered you?"

"Whoo! Be dodda, would your honour think Art ud tell a lie? Sure he read it. Aha!"

"An' what did he say, Art?"

"Whoo! Why, that he didn't know which of us had the least sense—you for sendin' a fool on a message, or me for deliverin' it."

"Was that all that happened?"

"No, sir. He said," added the fool, with bitter sarcasm, alluding to a duel in which the Squire's character had not come off with flying colours—"he said, sir, that whin you have another challenge to fight, you may get sick agin for threepence."

This having been the manner in which the Squire was said to have evaded the duel, it is unnecessary to say that Art's readiness to refresh his memory on the subject prevented him from being received at the big house in future.

Reader, remember that we only intended to give you a sketch of Phelim O'Toole's courtship; we will, however, go so far beyond our original plan as to apprise you of his fate.

When it became known in the parish that he was in gaol, under a charge of felony, Sally Flattery abandoned all hopes of securing him as a husband. The housekeeper felt suitable distress, and hoped, should the poor boy be acquitted, that "he might hould up his head wid any o' them." Phelim, through the agency of his father, succeeded in getting ten guineas from her, to pay the lawyers for defending him, not one penny of which he applied to the purpose for which he obtained it. The expenses of his defence were drawn from the Ribbon-boy fund; and the Irish reader cannot forget the elegant and pathetic appeal made by his counsel to the jury on his behalf, and the strength with which the fact of his being the whole support of a helpless father and mother was stated. The appeal, however, was ineffectual; worthy Phelim was convicted, and sentenced to transportation for life. When his old acquaintances heard the nature of his destiny, they remembered the two prophecies that had been so often uttered concerning him. One of them was certainly fulfilled to the letter—we mean that in which it was stated "that the greatest swaggerer among the girls generally comes to the wall at last." The other, though not literally accomplished, touched at least upon the spirit; transportation for life ranks next to hanging.

We cannot avoid mentioning a fact connected with Phelim which came to light while he remained in prison. By incessant trouble he was prevailed upon, or rather compelled, to attend the prison school, and on examining him touching his religious knowledge, it appeared that he was ignorant of the plainest truths of Christianity; that he knew not how or by whom the Christian religion had been promulgated, nor, indeed, any other moral truth connected with revelation.

Immediately after his transportation Larry took to drink, and his mother to begging, for she had no other means of living. In this mode of life the husband was soon compelled to join her. They are both mendicants, and Sheelah now appears sensible of the error in their manner of bringing Phelim up.

"Ah! Larry," she is sometimes heard to say, "I doubt that we wor wrong for flyin' in the face o' God because He didn't give us childher. An' when it plased Him to grant us a son, we oughtn't to've spoiled him by over-indulgence, an' by lettin' him have his own head in everything, as we did. If we had sint him to school, an' larned him to work, an' corrected him when he desarved it, instead of laughin' at his lies, an' misbehaviour, and his oaths, as if they wor sport—ay, an' abusin' the nabours when they'd complain of him, or tell us what he was—ay! if we had, it's a credit an' a comfort he'd be to us now, an' not a shame an' a disgrace an' an affliction. We made our own bed, Larry, an' now we must lie down an it. An' God help us! We made *his* bed too, poor boy, an' a bad one it is. God forgive us! But, anyhow, my heart's breakin', for, bad as he was, sure we haven't him to look upon!"

"Thrue," replied Larry. "Still he was game an' 'cute to the last. Biddy Doran's ten guineas will sarve him *beyant*, poor fellow. But sure the 'boys' kep' their word to him, anyhow, in regard of shootin' Foodle Flattery. Myself was never betther plased in my life than to hear that he got the slugs into his heart, the villain!"

THE THREE TASKS

OR, THE LITTLE HOUSE UNDER THE HILL

EVERY person in the parish knows the purty knoll that rises above the Routing Burn, some few miles from the renowned town of Knockimdowny, which, as all the world must allow, wants only houses and inhabitants to be as big a place as the great town of Dublin itself. At the foot of his little hill, just under the shelter of a dacent pebble of a rock, something about the bulk of half a dozen churches, one would be apt to see—if they knew how to look sharp, otherwise they mightn't be able to make it out from the grey rock above it, except by the smoke that ris from the chimbley — Nancy Magennis's little cabin, snug and cosy with its corrag,[1] or ould man of branches, standing on the windy side of the door, to keep away the blast.

" Upon my word, it was a dacent little residence in its own way, and so was Nancy herself, for that matther; for, though a poor widdy, she was very punctwell in paying for Jack's schooling, as I often heard ould Terry M'Phaudeen say, who tould me the story. Jack, indeed, grew up a fine slip; and, for hurling, football playing, and lepping, hadn't his likes in the five quarters of the parish. It's he that knew how to handle a spade and a raping-hook, and, what was betther nor all that, he was kind and tindher to his poor ould mother, and would let her want for nothing. Before he'd go to his day's work in the morning, he'd be sure to bring home from the clear spring-well that ran out of the other side of the rock, a pitcher of water to serve her for the day; nor would he forget to bring in a good creel of turf from the snug little peat-

---

[1] The *Corrag* is a roll of branches tied together with green, and used for the purposes mentioned in the story. It is six feet high, and much thicker than a sack, and is changed to either side of the door, according to the direction from which the wind blows.

97

stack that stood, thatched with rushes, before the door, and leave it in the corner, beside the fire ; so that she had nothing to do but put over her hand, without rising off her sate, and put down a sod when she wanted it.

"Nancy, on her part, kept Jack very clane and comfortable : his linen, though coorse, was always a good colour ; his working clothes tidily mended at all times ; and when he'd have occasion to put on his good coat to work in for the first time, Nancy would sew on the forepart of each sleeve a stout patch of ould cloth, to keep them from being worn by the spade ; so that when she'd rip these off them every Saturday night they would look as new and fresh as if he hadn't been working in them at all, at all.

"Then, when Jack came home in the winter nights, it would do your heart good to see Nancy sitting at her wheel, singing, 'Stachan Varagah,' or 'Peggy Na Laveen,' beside a purty clear fire, with a small pot of Murphys boiling on it for their supper, or laid up in a wooden dish, comfortably covered with a clane *praskeen*, on the well-swept hearthstone ; whilst the quiet, dancing blaze might be seen blinking in the nice earthen plates and dishes that stood over against the side wall of the house. Just before the fire you might see Jack's stool waiting for him to come home ; and, on the other side, the brown cat washing her face with her paws, or sitting beside the dog that lay asleep, quite happy and continted, purring her song, and now and then looking over at Nancy, with her eyes half shut, as much as to say, 'Catch a happier pair nor we are, Nancy, if you can.'

"Sitting quietly on the roost above the door were Dickey the cock, and half a dozen hens, that kept this honest pair in eggs and *egg-milk* for the best part of the year—besides enabling Nancy to sell two or three clutches of March-birds every season, to help to buy wool for Jack's big coat and her own grey-beard gown and striped red and blue petticoat.

"To make a long story short, no two could be more comfortable, considering everything. But, indeed, Jack was always obsarved to have a dacent, ginteel turn with him : for he'd scorn to see a bad gown on his mother, or a broken Sunday coat on himself ; and instead of drinking his little earning in a sheebeen house, and then eating his praties dry, he'd take care to have something to kitchen[1] them; so that he was not only snug and dacent of a Sunday, regarding wearables, but so well fed and rosy that the point of a rush would take a drop of blood out of his cheek.[2] Then he was the comeliest and best-looking young man in the parish, could tell lots of droll stories, and sing scores of merry songs, that would make you split your sides with downright laughing; and when a wake or a dance would happen to be in the neighbourhood, maybe there wouldn't be many a sly look out from the purty girls for pleasant Jack Magennis.

"In this way lived Jack and his mother, as happy and continted as two lords; except now and thin that Jack would feel a little consarn for not being able to lay past anything for the sore foot,[3] or that might enable him to think of marrying; for he was beginning to look about him for a wife— and why not, to be sure? But he was prudent, for all that, and didn't wish to bring a wife and small family into poverty and hardship without means to support them, as too many do.

"It was one fine frosty, moonlight night—the sky was without a cloud, and the stars all blinking that it would delight anybody's heart to look at them, when Jack was crassing a bog that lay a few fields beyant his own cabin. He was just crooning the 'Humours of Glin,' in to himself, and thinking that it was a very hard case that he couldn't save anything at all, at all, to help him to the wife—when, on coming down a bank in the middle of the bog, he saw a dark-looking man leaning against a clamp of turf, and a black dog, with a pipe of tobacky in his mouth, sitting at his ase beside him, and he smoking as sober as a judge. Jack, however, had a stout heart, bekase his conscience was clear, and, barring being a little daunted, he wasn't very much afeard. 'Who is this coming down toardst us?' said the black-favoured man, as he saw Jack approaching them. 'It's Jack Magennis,' says the dog, making answer, and taking the pipe out of his mouth with his right paw, and after puffing away

---

[1] Condiment or flavour.

[2] This proverb, which is always used as above, but without being confined in its application to only one sex, is a general one in Ireland. In delicacy and beauty I think it inimitable.

[3] Accidents—future calamity of any kind, or old age.

the smoke, and rubbing the end of it against his left leg, exactly as a Christian (this day's Friday, the Lord stand betune us and harm) would do against his sleeve, giving it at the same time to his comrade—'It's Jack Magennis,' says the dog, 'honest Widow Magennis's dacent son.' 'The very man,' says the other, back to him, 'that I'd wish to sarve, out of a thousand.—Arrah, Jack Magennis, how is every tether-length of you?' says the ould fellow, putting the *furrawn*[1] on him—'and how is every bone in your body, Jack, my darling? I'll hould a thousand guineas,' says he, pointing to a great big bag that lay beside him, 'and that's only the tenth part of what's in this bag, Jack, that you're just going to be in luck to-night, above all nights in the year!'

"'And may worse never happen you, Jack, *ma bouchal*,' says the dog, putting in his tongue, then wagging his tail, and houlding out his paw to shake hands with Jack.

"'Gintlemen,' says Jack, never minding to give the dog his hand, bekase he heard it wasn't safe to touch the likes of him—'Gintlemen,' says he, 'ye're sitting far from the fire this frosty night.'

"'Why, that's true, Jack,' answers the ould fellow; 'but if we're sitting far from the fire, we're sitting very near the makins of it, man alive.' So, with this, he pulls the bag of goold over to him, that Jack might know by the jingle of the shiners what was in it.

"'Jack,' says dark-face, 'there's some born with a silver ladle in their mouth, and others with a wooden spoon; and if you'll just sit down on the one end of this clamp with me, and take a hand at the "five-and-ten,"' pulling out, as he spoke, a deck of cards, 'you may be a made man for the remainder of your life.'

"'Sir,' says Jack, 'with submission, both yourself and this cur—I mane,' says he, not wishing to give the dog offence—'both yourself and this dacent gintleman with the tail and claws upon him, have the advantage of me, in respect of knowing my name; for, if I don't mistake,' says he, putting

---

[1] That frank, cordial manner of address which brings strangers suddenly to intimacy.

his hand to his *caubeen*, 'I never had the pleasure of seeing either of ye before.'

" ' Never mind that,' says the dog, taking back the pipe from the other, and clapping it in his mouth; ' we're both your well-wishers, anyhow, and it's now your own fault if you're not a rich man.'

" Jack, by this time, was beginning to think that they might be after wishing to throw luck in his way; for he had often heard of men being made up entirely by the fairies till there was no end to their wealth.

" ' Jack,' says the black man, ' you had better be sed by us for this bout—upon the honour of a gintleman we wish you well. However, if you don't choose to take the ball at the right hop, another may, and you're welcome to toil all your life, and die a beggar afther.'

" ' Upon my reputation, what he says is true, Jack,' says the dog, in his turn; ' the lucky minute of your life is come; let it pass without doing what them that wishes your mother's son well desire you, and you'll die in a ditch.'

" ' And what am I to do,' says Jack, ' that's to make me so rich all of a sudden ? '

" ' Why, only to sit down and take a game of cards with myself,' says black-brow, ' that's all, and I'm sure it's not much.'

" ' And what is it to be for ? ' Jack inquires, ' for I have no money—tare-nation to the rap itself's in my company.'

" ' Well, you have yourself,' says the dog, putting up his fore-claw along his nose, and winking at Jack, ' you have yourself, man—don't be faint-hearted—he'll bet the contents of this bag ; ' and with that the ould thief gave it another great big shake, to make the guineas jingle again. ' It's ten thousand guineas in hard gould ; if he wins, you're to sarve him for a year and a day ; and if he loses, you're to have the bag.'

" ' And the money that's in it,' says Jack, wishing, you see, to make a sure bargain, anyhow.

" ' Ev'ry penny,' answered the ould chap, ' if you win it ; and there's fifty to one in your favour.'

" By this time the dog had got into a great fit of laughing at Jack's sharpness about the money. ' The money that's in it, Jack,' says he, and he took the pipe out of his mouth, and laughed till he brought on a hard fit of coughing; 'oh, by this and by that,' says he, 'but that bates Bannagher! and you're to get it ev'ry penny, you thief of the world, if you win it;' but for all that he seemed to be laughing at something that Jack wasn't up to.

"At any rate, surely, they palavered Jack betune them, until he sot down and consinted. 'Well,' says he, scratching his head, 'why, worse nor lose I can't, so here goes for one trial at the shiners, anyhow!'

"'Now,' says the obscure gintleman, just whin the first card was in his hand, ready to be laid down, 'you're to sarve me for a year and a day if I win; and if I lose, you shall have all the money in the bag.'

"'Exactly,' says Jack, and just as he said the word he saw the dog putting the pipe in his pocket, and turning his head away for fraid Jack would see him breaking his sides laughing. At last, when he got his face sobered, he looks at Jack, and says, 'Surely, Jack, if you win, you must get all the money in the bag; and, upon my reputation, you may build castles in the air with it, you'll be so rich.'

"This plucked up Jack's courage a little, and to work they went; but how could it end otherwise than Jack to lose betune two such knowing schemers as they soon turned out to be? For what do you think, but as Jack was beginning the game, the dog tips him a wink, laying his fore-claw along his nose, as before, as much as to say, 'Watch me, and you'll win'—turning round, at the same time, and showing Jack a nate little looking-glass that was set in his oxther, in which Jack saw, dark as it was, the spots of all the other fellow's cards, as he thought, so that he was cock sure of bating him. But they were a pair of downright knaves, anyhow; for Jack, by playing to the cards that he saw in the looking-glass, instead of to them the other held in his hand, lost the game and the money. In short, he saw that he was blarnied and chated by them both; and when the game was up he plainly tould them as much.

"'What, you scoundrel!' says the black fellow, starting up and catching him by the collar, 'dare you go for to impache my honour?'

"'Leather him if he says a word,' says the dog, running over on his hind legs, and laying his shut paw upon Jack's nose. 'Say another word, you rascal,' says he, 'and I'll down you;' with this the ould fellow gives him another shake.

"'I don't blame you so much,' says Jack to him, 'it was the looking-glass that desaved me; that cur's nothing but a blackleg.'

"'What looking-glass, you knave you?' says dark-face, giving him a fresh haul.

"'Why, the one I saw under the dog's oxther,' replied Jack.

"'Under my oxther! you swindling rascal,' replied the dog, giving him a pull by the other side of the collar; 'did ever any honest pair of gintlemen hear the like?—but he only wants to break through the agreement; so let us turn him at once into an ass, and then he'll break no more bargains, nor strive to take in honest men and win their money. Me a blackleg!' So saying, the dark fellow drew his two hands over Jack's jaws, and in a twinkling there was a pair of ass's ears growing up out of his head. When Jack found this, he knew that he wasn't in good hands; so he thought it best to get himself as well out of the scrape as possible.

"'Gintlemen, be aisy,' says he, 'and let us understand one another. I'm very willing to sarve you for a year and a day, but I've one request to ax, and it's this: I've a helpless ould mother at home, and if I go with you now she'll break her heart with grief first, and starve afterwards. Now, if your honour will give me a year to work hard, and lay in provision to support her while I'm away, I'll serve you with all the veins of my heart—for a bargain's a bargain.'

"With this the dog gave his companion a pluck by the skirt, and, after some chat together, that Jack didn't hear, they came back and said they would comply with his wishes that far; 'so, on to-morrow twelvemonth, Jack,' says the dark fellow, 'the dog here will come to your mother's, and if you follow him he'll bring you safe to my castle.'

"'Very well, your honour,' says Jack; 'but as dogs resemble one another so much, how will I know him whin he comes?'

"'Why,' answers the other, 'he'll have a green ribbon about his neck, and a pair of Wellington boots on his hind legs.'

"'That's enough, sir,' says Jack, 'I can't mistake him in

103

that dress, so I'll be ready; but gintlemen, if it would be plasing to you both, I'd every bit as soon not go home with these,' and he handled the brave pair of ears he had got, as he spoke. 'The truth is, gintlemen, I'm deluding enough without them; and as I'm so modest, you persave, why, if you'd take them away you'd oblige me!'

" To this they had no objection, and during that year Jack wrought night and day, that he might be able to lave as much provision with his poor mother as would support her in his absence; and when the morning came that he was to bid her farewell he went down on his two knees and got her blessing. He then left her with tears in his eyes, and promised to come back the very minute his time would be up. 'Mother,' says he, 'be kind to your little family here, and feed them well, as they are all you'll have to keep you company till you see me again.'

" His mother then stuffed his pockets with bread, till they stuck out behind him, and gave him a crooked sixpence for luck; after which he got his staff, and was just ready to tramp, when, sure enough, he spies his ould friend the dog, with the green ribbon about his neck, and the Wellington boots upon his hind legs. He didn't go in, but waited on the outside till Jack came out. They then set off, but no one knows how far they travelled, till they reached the dark gintleman's castle, who appeared very glad to see Jack, and gave him a hearty welcome.

" The next day, in consequence of his long journey, he was ax'd to do nothing; but in the coorse of the evening the dark chap brought him into a long, frightful room, where there were three hundred and sixty-five hooks sticking out of the wall, and on every hook but one a man's head. When Jack saw this agreeable sight, his dinner began to quake within him; but he felt himself still worse when his master pointed to the empty hook, saying, ' Now, Jack, your business to-morrow is to clane out a stable that wasn't claned for the last seven years, and if you don't have it finished before dusk —do you see that hook?'

" ' Ye—yes,' replied Jack, hardly able to spake. ' Well, if you don't have it finished before dusk your head will be hanging on that hook as soon as the sun sets.'

104

"'Very well, your honour,' replied Jack, scarcely knowing what he said, or he wouldn't have said 'very well' to such a bloody-minded intention, anyhow — 'Very well,' says he, 'I'll do my best, and all the world knows that the best can do no more.'

"Whilst this discourse was passing betune them, Jack happened to look at the upper end of the room, and there he saw one of the beautifullest faces that ever was seen on a woman, looking at him through a little panel that was in the wall. She had a white, snowy forehead—such eyes, and cheeks, and teeth, that there's no coming up to them; and the clusters of dark hair that hung about her beautiful temples!—by the laws, I'm afeard of falling in love with her myself, so I'll say no more about her, only that she would charm the heart of a wheel-barrow. At any rate, in spite of all the ould fellow could say — heads, and hooks, and all, Jack couldn't help throwing an eye now and then to the panel; and to tell the truth, if he had been born to riches and honour, it would be hard to fellow him for a good face and a good figure.

"'Now, Jack,' said his master, 'go and get your supper, and I hope you'll be able to perform your task—if not, off goes your head.'

"'Very well, your honour,' says Jack, again scratching it in the hoith of perplexity, 'I must only do what I can.'

"The next morning Jack was up with the sun, if not before him, and hard at his task ; but before breakfast-time he lost all heart, and little wonder he should, poor fellow, bekase, for every one shovelful he'd throw out, there would come three more in : so that instead of making his task less, according as he got on, it became greater. He was now in the greatest dilemmy, and didn't know how to manage, so he was driven at last to such an amplush, that he had no other shift for employment, only to sing 'Paudeen O'Rafferty' out of mere vexation, and dance the hornpipe trebling step to it, cracking his fingers, half mad, through the stable. Just in the middle of this tantrum, who comes to the dour to call him to his breakfast but the beautiful crathur he saw the evening before peeping at him through the panel. At this minute Jack had so hated himself by the dancing that his handsome face was in a fine glow entirely.

"'I think,' said she to Jack, with one of her own sweet smiles, 'that this is an odd way of performing your task.'

"'Och, thin, 'tis you that may say that,' replies Jack; 'but it's myself that's willing to have my head hung up any day, just for one sight of you, you darling.'

"'Where did you come from?' asked the lady, with another smile that bate the first all to nothing.

"'Where did I come from, is it?' answered Jack; 'why, death-alive! did you never hear of ould Ireland, my jewel? —hem—I mane, plase your ladyship's honour.'

"'No,' she answered; 'where is that country?'

"'Och, by the honour of an Irishman,' says Jack, 'that takes the shine!—not heard of Erin—the Imerald Isle—the Jim of the ocean, where all the men are brave and honourable, and all the women—hem—I mane the ladies—chaste and beautiful?'

"'No,' said she; 'not a word: but if I stay longer I may get you into blame—come into your breakfast, and I'm sorry to find that you have done so little at your task. Your master's a man that always acts up to what he threatens; and, if you have not this stable cleared out before dusk, your head will be taken off your shoulders this night.'

"'Why, thin,' says Jack, 'my beautiful darl—plase your honour's ladyship—if he hangs it up, will you do me the favour, *acushla machree*, to turn my head toardst that same panel where I saw a sartin fair face that. I wea't mintion; and if you do, let me alone for watching a sartin purty face I'm acquainted with.'

"'What means *cushla machree*?' inquired the lady, as she turned to go away.

"'It manes that you're the pulse of my heart, *avourneen*, plase your ladyship's reverence,' says Jack.

"'Well,' said the lovely crathur, 'any time you speak to me in future, I would rather you would omit terms of honour, and just call me after the manner of your own country; instead, for instance, of calling me your ladyship, I would be better pleased if you called me *cushla*—something'——

"'*Cushla machree, ma vourneen*—the pulse of my heart—my darling,' said Jack, consthering it (the thief) for her, for fraid she wouldn't know it well enough.

"'Yes,' she replied, '*cushla machree;* well, as I can pronounce it, *acushla machree*, will you come into your breakfast?' said the darling, giving Jack a smile that would be enough, any day, to do up the heart of an Irishman. Jack accordingly went after her, thinking of nothing except herself; but on going in he could see no sign of her, so he sat down to his breakfast, though a single ounce, barring a couple of pounds of beef, the poor fellow couldn't ate at that bout for thinking of her.

"Well, he went again to his work, and thought he'd have better luck; but it was still the ould game—three shovelfuls would come in for ev'ry one he'd throw out; and now he began, in earnest, to feel something about his heart that he didn't like, bekase he couldn't, for the life of him, help thinking of the three hundred and sixty-four heads and the empty hook. At last he gave up the work entirely, and took it into his head to make himself scarce from about the ould fellow's castle altogether; and without more to do he set off, never saying as much as 'good-bye' to his master; but he hadn't got as far as the lower end of the yard when his ould friend, the dog, steps out of a kennel, and meets him full butt in the teeth.

"'So, Jack,' says he, 'you're going to give us leg bail, I see; but walk back with yourself, you *spalpeen*, this minute, and join your work, or if you don't,' says he, it will be worse for your health. I'm not so much your enemy now as I was, bekase you have a friend in coort that you know nothing about; so just do whatever you are bid, and keep never minding.'

"Jack went back with a heavy heart, as you may be sure, knowing that whenever the black cur began to blarney him there was no good to come in his way. He accordingly went into the stable, but consuming to the hand's turn he did, knowing it would be only useless; for, instead of clearing it out, he'd be only filling it.

"It was now near dinner-time, and Jack was very sad and sorrowful—as how could he be otherwise, poor fellow, with such a bloody-minded ould chap to dale with?—when up comes the darling of the world again to call him to his dinner.

" 'Well, Jack,' says she, with her white arms so beautiful, and her dark clusters tossed about by the motion of the walk, 'how are you coming on at your task?'

" 'How am I coming on, is it? Och, thin,' says Jack, giving a good-humoured smile through the frown that was on his face, 'plase your lady—*acushla machree*—it's all over with me; for I've still the same story to tell, and off goes my head, as sure as it's on my shoulders, this blessed night.'

" 'That would be a pity, Jack,' says she, 'for there are worse heads on worse shoulders; but will you give me the shovel?'

" 'Will I give *you* the shovel, is it? Och, thin, wouldn't I be a right big baste to do the likes of that, anyhow?' says Jack. 'What! *avourneen dheelish!* to stand up with myself, and let this hard shovel into them beautiful, soft, white hands of your own! Faix, my jewel, if you knew but all, my mother's son's not the man to do such a disgraceful turn as to let a lady like you take the shovel out of his hand, and he standing with his mouth under his nose looking at you—not myself, *avourneen!* we have no such ungenteel manners as that in our country.'

" 'Take my advice, Jack,' says she, pleased in her heart at what Jack said, for all she didn't purtend it—'give me the shovel, and, depend upon it, I'll do more in a short time to clear the stable than you would for years.'

" 'Why, thin, *avourneen,* it goes to my heart to refuse you; but, for all that, may I never see yesterday if a taste of it will go into your purty white fingers,' says the thief, praising her to her face all the time; 'my head may go off any day, and welcome, but death before dishonour. Say no more, darling; but tell your father I'll be in to my dinner immediately.'

" Notwithstanding all this, by jingo the lady would not be put off. Like a ra-al woman, she'd have her way. So, on telling Jack that she didn't intend to work with the shovel at all, at all, but only to take it for a minute in her hand, at long last he gave it to her. She then struck it three times on the threshel of the door, and, giving it back into his hand, tould him to try what he could do. Well, sure enough, now there was a change; for instead of three shovelfuls coming in, as before, when he threw one out, there went nine more along with it. Jack, in coorse, couldn't do less than thank the lovely crathur for her assistance; but when he raised his head to speak to her she was gone. I needn't say, howsom-ever, that he went in to his dinner with a light heart and a murdhering appetite; and when the ould fellow axed him how he was coming on, Jack tould him that he was doing gloriously. 'Remember the empty hook, Jack,' said he. 'Never fear, your honour,' answered Jack; 'if I don't finish my task, you may bob my head off any time.'

"Jack now went out, and was a short time getting through his job, for before the sun set it was finished; and he came into the kitchen, ate his supper, and, sitting down before the fire, sung 'Love among the Roses' and the 'Black Joke,' to vex the ould fellow.

"This was one task over, and his head was safe for that bout; but that night, before he went to bed, his master called him upstairs, brought him into the bloody room, and gave him his orders for the next day. 'Jack,' says he, 'I have a wild filly that has never been caught, and you must go to my demesne to-morrow and catch her, or if you don't—look there,' says the big blackguard, 'on that hook it hangs before to-morrow if you haven't her before sunset in the stable that you claned yesterday.' 'Very well, your honour,' says Jack carelessly; 'I'll do everything in my power, and if I fail I can't help it.'

"The next morning Jack was out with a bridle in his hand, going to catch the filly. As soon as he got into the demesne, sure enough, there she was in the middle of a green field, grazing quite at her ase. When Jack saw this he went over towards her, houlding out his hat, as if it was full of oats; but he kept the hand that had the bridle in it behind his back, for fraid she'd see it and make off. Well, my dear, on he went till he was almost within grip of her, cock sure that he had nothing more to do than slip the bridle over her neck and secure her; but he made a bit of a mistake in his reckon-ing, for though she smelt and smoked about him, just as if she didn't care a feed of oats whether he caught her or not, yet when he boulted over to hould her fast, she was off like a shot, with her tail cocked, to the far end of the demesne, and Jack had to set off hot foot after her. All, however, was to no purpose; he couldn't come next or near her for the rest of the day, and there she kept coorsing about him, from one field to another, till he hadn't a blast of breath in his body.

"In this state was Jack when the beautiful crathur came out to call him home to his breakfast, walking, with the pretty small feet and light steps of her own, upon the green fields, so bright and beautiful, scarcely bending the grass and flowers as she went along, the darling.

"'Jack,' says she, 'I fear you have as difficult a task to-day as you had yesterday.'

"'Why, and it's you that may say that with your own purty mouth,' says Jack, says he; for out of breath and all as he was, he couldn't help giving her a bit of blarney, the rogue.

"'Well, Jack,' says she, 'take my advice, and don't tire yourself any longer by attempting to catch her; truth's best—I tell you, you could never do it. Come home to your breakfast, and when you return again, just amuse yourself as well as you can until dinner time.'

"'Och, och!' says Jack, striving to look, the sly thief, as if she had promised to help him—'I only wish I was a king, and, by the powers, I know who would be my queen, anyhow; for it's your own sweet lady—*savourneen dheelish*. I say, amn't I bound to you for a year and a day longer, for promising to give me a lift, as well as for what you done yesterday?'

"'Take care, Jack,' says she, smiling, however, at his ingenuity in striving to trap her into a promise; 'I don't think I made any promise of assistance.'

"'You didn't?' says Jack, wiping his face with the skirt of his coat; 'cause why?—you see pocket-handkerchiefs weren't invented in them times. 'Why, thin, may I never live to see yesterday, if there's not as much rale beauty in that smile that's divarting itself about them sweet breathing lips of yours and in them two eyes of light that's breaking both their hearts laughing at me this minute, as would encourage any poor fellow to expect a good turn from you—that is, whin you could do it without hurting or harming yourself; for it's he would be the right rascal that could take it if it would injure a silken hair of your head.'

"'Well,' said the lady, with another roguish smile, 'I shall call you home to your dinner, at all events.'

110

" When Jack went back from his breakfast he didn't slave himself after the filly any more, but walked about to view the demesne, and the avenues, and the green walks, and nice temples, and fish-ponds and rookeries, and everything, in short, that was worth seeing. Towards dinner-time, however, he began to have an eye to the way the sweet crathur was to come, and sure enough it's she that wasn't one minute late.

"'Well, Jack,' says she, 'I'll keep you no longer in doubt,' for the tender-hearted crathur saw that Jack, although he didn't wish to let an to her, was fretting every now and then about the odd hook and the bloody room—'So, Jack,' says she, 'although I didn't promise, yet I'll perform;' and with that she pulled a small ivory whistle out of her pocket, and gave three blasts on it that brought the wild filly up to her very hand, as quick as the wind. She then took the bridle, and threw it over the baste's neck, giving her up, at the same time, to Jack. 'You needn't fear now, Jack,' says she; 'you will find her as quiet as a lamb, and as tame as you wish : as a proof of it, just walk before her, and you will see she will follow you to any part of the field.'

" Jack, you may be sure, paid her as many and as sweet compliments as he could, and never heed one from his country for being able to say something toothsome to the ladies. At any rate, if he laid it on thick the day before, he gave her two or three additional coats this time, and the innocent soul went away smiling, as usual.

" When Jack brought the filly home, the dark fellow, his master, if dark before, was a perfect tundher-cloud this night : bedad, he was nothing less than near bursting with vexation, bekase the thieving ould sinner intended to have Jack's head upon the hook ; but he fell short in his reckoning now as well as before. Jack sung 'Love among the Roses' and the 'Black Joke,' to help him into better timper.

"'Jack,' says he, striving to make himself speak pleasant to him, 'you've got two difficult tasks over you; but you know the third time's the charm—take care of the next.'

"'No matter about that,' says Jack, speaking up to him stiff and stout, bekase, as the dog tould him, he knew he had a friend in coort ; 'let's hear what it is, anyhow.'

"'To-morrow, then,' says the other, 'you're to rob a crane's

111

nest on the top of a beech tree which grows in the middle of a little island in the lake that you saw, yesterday, in my demesne; you're to have neither boat, nor oar, nor any kind of conveyance, but just as you stand; and if you fail to bring me the eggs, or if you break one of them—look here!' says he, again pointing to the odd hook, for all this discourse took place in the bloody room.

"'Good again,' says Jack; 'if I fail, I know my doom.'

"'No, you don't, you *spalpeen*,' says the other, getting vexed with him entirely; 'for I'll roast you till you're half dead, and ate my dinner off you after; and, what is more than that, you blackguard, you must sing the "Black Joke" all the time for my amusement.'

"'Div'l fly away with you,' thought Jack, 'but you're fond .of music, you vagabond.'

"The next morning Jack was going round and round the lake, trying about the edge of it if he could find any place shallow enough to wade in; but he might as well go to wade the say, and, what was worse of all, if he attempted to swim, it would be like a tailor's goose—straight to the bottom; so he kept himself safe on dry land, still expecting a visit from the 'lovely crathur,' but, bedad, his good luck failed him for wanst; for, instead of seeing her coming over to him, so mild and sweet, who does he observe steering, at a dog's trot, but his ould friend the smoking cur. 'Confusion to that cur,' says Jack to himself; 'I know now there's some bad fortune before me, or he wouldn't be coming acrass me.'

"'Come home to your breakfast, Jack,' says the dog, walking up to him; 'it's breakfast-time.'

"'Ay,' says Jack, scratching his head; 'it's no great matter whether I do or not, for I bleeve my head's hardly worth a flat-dutch cabbage at the present speaking.'

"'Why, man, it was never worth so much,' says the baste, pulling out his pipe and putting it in his mouth, when it lit at once.

"'Take care of yourself,' says Jack, quite desperate—for he thought he was near the end of his tether—'take care of yourself, you dirty cur, or maybe I might take a gintleman's toe from the nape of your neck.'

"'You had better keep a straight tongue in your head,'

says four legs, 'while it's on your shoulders, or I'll break every bone in your skin. Jack, you're a fool,' says he, checking himself, and speaking kindly to him—'you're a fool; didn't I tell you the other day to do what you were bid, and keep never minding?'

"'Well,' thought Jack to himself, 'there's no use in making him any more my enemy than he is—particularly as I'm in such a hobble.'

"'You lie,' says the dog, as if Jack had spoken out to him, wherein he only thought the words to himself—'You lie,' says he; 'I'm not, nor never was, your enemy, if you knew but all.'

"'I beg your honour's pardon,' answers Jack, 'for being so smart with your honour; but, bedad, if you were in my case—if you expected your master to roast you alive—eat his dinner off your body—make you sing the "Black Joke" by way of music for him; and, to crown all, knew that your head was to be stuck upon a hook after—maybe you would be a little short in your temper as well as your neighbours.'

"'Take heart, Jack,' says the other, laying his fore-claw as knowingly as ever along his nose, and winking slyly at Jack; 'didn't I tell you that you have a friend in coort? The day's not past yet; so cheer up; who knows but there is luck before you still?'

"'Why, thin,' says Jack, getting a little cheerful, and wishing to crack a joke with him, 'but your honour's very fond of the pipe!'

"'Oh! don't you know, Jack,' says he, 'that that's the fashion at present among my tribe: sure, all my brother puppies smoke now, and a man might as well be out of the world as out of the fashion, you know.'

"When they drew near home they got quite thick entirely. 'Now,' says Jack, in a good-humoured way, 'if you can give me a lift in robbing this crane's nest, do; at any rate, I'm sure your honour won't be my enemy. I know you have too much good nature in your face to be one that wouldn't help a lame dog over a stile—that is,' says he, taking himself up for fear of offending the other, 'I'm sure you'd be always inclined to help the weak side.'

"'Thank you for the compliment,' says the dog; 'but didn't I tell you that you have a friend in coort?'

"When Jack went back to the lake, he could only sit and look sorrowfully at the tree, or walk about the edge of it, without being able to do anything else. He spent the whole day this-a-way till dinner-time, when what would you have of it but he sees the 'darling' coming out to him, as fair and as blooming as an angel. His heart, you may be sure, got up to his mouth, for he knew she would be apt to take him out of his difficulties. When she came up—

"'Now, Jack,' says she, 'there is not a minute to be lost, for I'm watched; and if it's discovered that I gave you any assistance we will be both destroyed.'

"'Oh, murther, *sheery!*' says Jack, 'fly back, *avourneen machree;* for, rather than anything should happen you, I'd lose fifty lives.'

"'No,' says she; 'I think I'll be able to get you over this, as well as the rest; so have a good heart and be faithful.'

"'That's it,' replied Jack—'that's it, *acushla*—my own correcthur to a shaving; I've a heart worth its weight in banknotes, and a more faithful boy isn't alive this day nor I am to yees all, ye darlings of the world.'

"She then pulled a small white wand out of her pocket, struck the lake, and there was the prettiest green ridge across it to the foot of the tree that ever eye beheld. 'Now,' says she, turning her back to Jack, and stooping down to do something that he couldn't see, 'take these, put them against the tree, and you will have steps to carry you to the top; but be sure, for your life and mine, not to forget any of them; if you do, my life will be taken to-morrow morning, for your master puts on my slippers with his own hands.'

"Jack was now going to swear that he would give up the whole thing, and surrender his head at once; but when he looked at her feet and saw no appearance of blood, he went over without more to do, and robbed the nest, taking down the eggs one by one, that he mightn't break them. There was no end to his joy as he secured the last egg. He instantly took down the toes, one after another, save and except the little one of the left foot, which, in his joy and hurry, he forgot entirely. He then returned by the green ridge to the shore, and according as he went along it melted away into the water behind him.

114

"'Jack,' says the charmer, 'I hope you forgot none of my toes.'

"'Is it me?' says Jack, quite sure that he had them all. 'Arrah, catch any one from my country makin' a blunder of that kind.'

"'Well,' says she, 'let us see.' So, taking the toes, she placed them on again, just as if they had never been off. But, lo and behold! on coming to the last of the left foot, it wasn't forthcoming. 'O Jack, Jack!' says she, 'you have destroyed me; to-morrow morning your master will notice the want of this toe, and that instant I'll be put to death.'

"'Lave that to me,' says Jack; 'by the powers, you won't lose a drop of your darling blood for it. Have you got a penknife about you? and I'll soon show you how you won't.'

"'What do you want with the knife?' she inquired.

"'What do I want with it?—why, to give you the best toe on both my feet, for the one I lost on you. Do you think I'd suffer you to want a toe, and I have ten thumping ones at your sarvice!—I'm not the man, you beauty, you, for such a shabby trick as that comes to.'

"'But you forget,' says the lady, who was a little cooler than Jack, 'that none of yours would fit me.'

"'And must you die to-morrow, *acushla?*' asked Jack, in desperation.

"'As sure as the sun rises,' answered the lady; 'for your master would know at once that it was by my toes the nest was robbed.'

"'By the powers,' observed Jack, 'he's one of the greatest ould vag—I mane, isn't he a terrible man, out and out, for a father?'

"'Father!' says the darling—'he's not my father, Jack; he only wishes to marry me, and if I'm not able to outdo him before three days more, it's decreed that he must have me.'

"When Jack heard this, surely the Irishman must come out; there he stood, and began to wipe his eyes with the skirt of his coat, making as if he was crying, the thief of the world.

"'What's the matter with you?' she asked.

"'Ah!' says Jack, 'you darling, I couldn't find in my heart to desave you: for I have no way at home to keep a lady like you, in proper style, at all, at all; I would only bring you into poverty; and since you wish to know what ails me, I'm vexed that I'm not rich for your sake, and next, that that thieving ould villain's to have you; and, by the powers, I'm crying for both these misfortunes together.'

"The lady couldn't help being touched and plaised with Jack's tinderness and ginerosity; so, says she, 'Don't be cast down, Jack; come or go what will, I won't marry him—I'd die first. Do you go home, as usual; but take care and don't sleep at all this night. Saddle the wild filly—meet me under the whitethorn bush at the end of the lawn, and we'll both leave him for ever. If you're willing to marry me, don't let poverty distress you, for I have more money than we'll know what to do with.'

"Jack's voice now began to tremble in earnest, with downright love and tinderness, as good right it had; so he promised to do everything just as she bid him, and then went home with a dacent appetite enough to his supper.

"You may be sure the ould fellow looked darker and grimmer than ever at Jack; but what could he do? Jack had done his duty; so he sat before the fire, and sung 'Love among the Roses' and the 'Black Joke,' with a stouter and lighter heart than ever, while the black chap could have seen him skivered.

"When midnight came, Jack, who kept a hawk's eye to the night, was at the hawthorn with the wild filly, saddled and all—more betoken, she wasn't a bit wild then, but as tame as a dog. Off they set, like *Erin-go-bragh*, Jack and the lady, and never pulled bridle till it was one o'clock next day, when they stopped at an inn and had some refreshment. They then took the road again, full speed; however, they hadn't gone far, when they heard a great noise behind them, and the tramp of horses galloping like mad. 'Jack,' says the darling, on hearing the hubbub, 'look behind you, and see what's this.'

"'Och! by the elevens,' says Jack, 'we're done at last; it's the dark fellow, and half the country, after us.'

"'Put your hand,' says she, 'in the filly's right ear, and tell me what you find in it.'

"'Nothing at all, at all,' says Jack, 'but a *wheeshy* bit of a dry stick.'

116

"'Throw it over your left shoulder,' says she, 'and see what will happen.'

"Jack did so at once, and there was a great grove of thick trees growing so close to one another that a dandy could scarcely get his arm betwixt them.

"'Now,' said she, 'we are safe for another day.'

"'Well,' said Jack, as he pushed on the filly, 'you're the jewel of the world, sure enough; and maybe it's you that won't live happy when we get to the Jim of the Ocean.'

"As soon as the dark-face saw what happened, he was obliged to scour the country for hatchets and hand-saws, and all kinds of sharp instruments, to hew himself and his men a passage through the grove. As the saying goes, many hands make light work, and, sure enough, it wasn't long till they had cleared a way for themselves, thick as it was, and set off with double speed after Jack and the lady.

"The next day, about one o'clock, he and she were after taking another small refreshment of roast-beef and porther, and pushing on, as before, when they heard the same tramping behind them, only it was ten times louder.

"'Here they are again,' says Jack; 'and I'm afeard they'll come up with us at last.'

"'If they do,' says she, 'they'll put us to death on the spot; but we must try somehow to stop them another day, if we can: search the filly's right ear again, and let me know what you find in it.'

"Jack pulled out a little three-cornered pebble, telling her that it was all he got.

"'Well,' says she, 'throw it over your left shoulder like the stick.'

"No sooner said than done; and there was a great chain of high, sharp rocks in the way of divil-face and all his clan. 'Now,' says she, 'we have gained another day.'

"'Tundher-and-turf!' says Jack, 'what's this for, at all, at all?—but wait till I get you in the Imerald Isle, for this, and if you don't enjoy happy days anyhow, why, I'm not sitting before you on this horse, by the same token that it's not a horse at all, but a filly though: if you don't get the hoith of good aiting and drinking—lashings of the best wine and whisky that the land can afford, my name's not Jack. We'll build a castle, and

117

you'll have upstairs and downstairs—a coach and six to ride in—lots of servants to attend on you, and full and plinty of everything; not to mintion—hem!—not to mintion that you'll have a husband that the fairest lady in the land might be proud of,' says he, stretching himself up in the saddle, and giving the filly a jag of the spurs, to show off a bit; although the coaxing rogue knew that the money which was to do all this was her own. At any rate, they spent the remainder of this day pleasantly enough, still moving on, though, as fast as they could. Jack, every now and then, would throw an eye behind, as if to watch their pursuers, wherein, if the truth was known, it was to get a peep at the beautiful glowing face and warm lips that were breathing all kinds of *fraagrancies* about him. I'll warrant he didn't envy the King upon his throne when he felt the honeysuckle of her breath, like the smell of Father Ned's orchard there of a May morning.

"When Fardorougha[1] found the great chain of rocks before him, you may set it down that he was likely to blow up with vexation; but, for all that, the first thing he blew up was the rocks; and that he might lose little or no time in doing it, he collected all the gunpowder and crowbars, spades and pickaxes, that could be found for miles about him, and set to it, working as if it was with inch of candle. For half a day there was nothing but boring and splitting, and driving of iron wedges, and blowing up pieces of rocks as big as little houses, until, by hard labour, they made a passage for themselves sufficient to carry them over. They then set off again, full speed; and great advantage they had over the poor filly that Jack and the lady rode on, for their horses were well rested, and hadn't to carry double, like Jack's. The next day they spied Jack and his beautiful companion just about a quarter of a mile before them.

"'Now,' says dark-brow, 'I'll make any man's fortune for ever that will bring me them two, either living or dead, but, if possible, alive; so, spur on, for whoever secures them is a made man—but, above all things, make no noise.'

"It was now divil take the hindmost among the bloody pack — every spur was red with blood, and every horse

---

[1] The dark man.

smoking. Jack and the lady were jogging on acrass a green field, not suspecting that the rest were so near them, and talking over the pleasant days they would spind together in Ireland, when they hears the hue-and-cry once more at their very heels.

"'Quick as lightning, Jack,' says she, 'or we're lost—the right ear and the left shoulder, like thought—they're not three lengths of the filly from us!'

"But Jack knew his business; for just as a long, grim-looking villain, with a great rusty rapier in his hand, was within a single leap of them, and quite sure of either killing or making prisoners of them both, Jack flings a little drop of green water, that he got in the filly's ear, over his left shoulder, and in an instant there was a deep, dark gulf, filled with black, pitchy-looking water, between them. The lady now desired Jack to pull up the filly a bit, till they would see what would become of the dark fellow; but, just as they turned round, the ould nager set spurs to his horse, and, in a fit of desperation, plunged himself, horse and all, into the gulf, and was never seen or heard of more. The rest that were with him went home, and began to quarrel about his wealth, and kept murdering and killing one another, until a single vagabond of them wasn't left alive to enjoy it.

"When Jack saw what happened, and that the bloodthirsty ould villain got what he desarved so richly, he was as happy as a prince, and ten times happier than most of them as the world goes, and she was every bit as delighted. 'We have nothing more to fear,' said the darling that put them all down so cleverly, seeing she was but a woman; but, bedad, it's she was the right sort of a woman: 'all our dangers are now over—at least, all yours are; regarding myself,' says she, 'there is a trial before me yet, and that trial, Jack, depends upon your faithfulness and constancy.'

"'On me, is it? Och, then, murder! isn't it a poor case entirely, that I have no way of showing you that you may depend your life upon me, only by telling you so?'

"'I do depend upon you,' says she—'and now, as you love me, do not, when the trial comes, forget her that saved you out of so many troubles, and made you such a great and wealthy man.

"The foregoing part of this Jack could well understand; but the last part of it, making collusion to the wealth, was a little dark, he thought, bekase he hadn't fingered any of it at that time; still, he knew she was truth to the backbone, and wouldn't desave him. They hadn't travelled much farther, when Jack snaps his fingers, with a 'Whoo! by the powers, there it is, my darling—there it is, at long last!'

"'There is what, Jack?' said she, surprised, as well she might, at his mirth and happiness—'There is what?' says she.

"'Cheer up,' says Jack; 'there it is, my darling—the Shannon!—as soon as we get to the other side of it we'll be in ould Ireland once more.'

"There was no end to Jack's good-humour when he crossed the Shannon; and she was not a bit displased to see him so happy. They had now no enemies to fear, were in a civilised country, and among green fields and well-bred people. In this way they travelled at their ase, till they came within a few miles of the town of Knockimdowny, near which Jack's mother lived.

"'Now, Jack,' says she, 'I tould you that I would make you rich. You know the rock beside your mother's cabin; in the east end of that rock there is a loose stone, covered over with grey moss, just two feet below the cleft out of which the hanging rowan tree grows—pull that stone out, and you will find more goold than would make a duke. Neither speak to any person, nor let any living thing touch your lips till you come back to me, or you'll forget that you ever saw me, and I'll be left poor and friendless in a strange country.'

"'Why, thin, *manim asthee hu*,' says Jack, 'but the best way to guard against that, is to touch your own sweet lips at the present time,' says he, giving her a smack that you'd hear, of a calm evening, acrass a couple of fields. Jack set off to touch the money with such speed that when he fell he scarcely waited to rise again; he was soon at the rock, anyhow, and, without either doubt or disparagement, there was a cleft of ra-al goolden guineas, as fresh as daisies. The first thing he did, after he had filled his pockets with them, was to look if his mother's cabin was to the fore; and there surely it was, as snug as ever, with the same dacent column of smoke rowling from the chimbley.

"'Well,' thought he, 'I'll just stale over to the door-cheek, and peep in to get one sight of my poor mother; then I'll throw her in a handful of these guineas, and take to my scrapers.'

"Accordingly, he stole up at a half-bend to the door, and was just going to take a peep in, when out comes the little dog Trig, and begins to leap and fawn upon him, as if it would eat him. The mother, too, came running out to see what was the matter, when the dog made another spring up about Jack's neck, and gave his lips the slightest lick in the world with its tongue, the crathur was so glad to see him : the next minute Jack forgot the lady as clane as if he had never seen her ; but, if he forgot her, catch him at forgetting the money—not he, *avick !*—that stuck to him like pitch.

"When the mother saw who it was, she flew to him, and, clasping her arms about his neck, hugged him till she wasn't worth three half-pence. After Jack sot a while, he made a trial to let her know what had happened him, but he disremembered it all, except having the money in the rock, so he up and tould her that, and a glad woman she was to hear of his good fortune. Still, he kept the place where the goold was to himself, having been often forbid by her ever to trust a woman with a sacret when he could avoid it.

"Now, everybody knows what changes the money makes, and Jack was no exception to this ould saying. In a few years he had built himself a fine castle, with three hundred and sixty-four windies in it, and he would have added another, to make one for every day in the year, only that that would be equal to the number in the King's palace, and the Lord of the Black Rod would be sent to take his head off, it being high thrason for a subject to have as many windies in his house as the King. However, Jack, at any rate, had enough of them ; and he that couldn't be happy with three hundred and sixty-four wouldn't desarve to have three hundred and sixty-five. Along with all this, he bought coaches and carriages, and didn't get proud, like many other beggarly upstarts, but took especial good care of his mother, whom he dressed in silks and satins, and gave her nice nourishing food that was fit for an ould woman in her condition. He also got great teachers, men of deep larning, from Dublin, acquainted with all subjects; and, as his own abilities were bright, he soon became a very great scholar entirely, and was able, in the long-run, to outdo all his tutherers.

"In this way he lived for some years—was now a man of great larning himself—could spake the seven langwidges, and it would delight your ears to hear how high-flown and Englified he could talk. All the world wondered where he got his wealth; but, as he was kind and charitable to every one that stood in need of assistance, the people said that, wherever he got it, it couldn't be in better hands. At last he began to look about him for a wife, and the only one in that part of the country that would be at all fit for him was the Honourable Miss Bandbox, the daughter of a nobleman in the neighbourhood. She, indeed, flogged all the world for beauty; but it was said that she was proud and fond of wealth, though, God He knows, she had enough of that, anyhow. Jack, however, saw none of this; for she was cunning enough to smile, and simper, and look pleasant, whenever he'd come to her father's. Well, begad, from one thing and one word to another, Jack thought it was best to make up to her at wanst, and try if she'd accept of him for a husband; accordingly, he put the word to her, like a man, and she, making as if she was blushing, put her fan before her face and made no answer. Jack, however, wasn't to be daunted; for he knew two things worth knowing when a man goes to look for a wife: the first is—that 'faint heart never won fair lady;' and the second—that 'silence gives consint.' He therefore spoke up to her in fine English, for it's he that knew how to speak now, and, after a little more fanning and blushing, by jingo, she consinted. Jack then broke the matter to her father, who was as fond of money as the daughter, and only wanted to grab at him for the wealth.

"When the match was a-making, says ould Bandbox to Jack, 'Mr. Magennis,' says he (for nobody called him Jack now but his mother), 'these two things you must comply with, if you marry my daughter, Miss Gripsy: you must send away your mother from about you, and pull down the cabin in which you and she used to live; Gripsy says that they would jog her memory consarning your low birth and former poverty. She's nervous and high-spirited, Mr.

122

Magennis, and declares upon her honour that she couldn't bear the thoughts of having the delicacy of her feeling offinded by these things.'

"'Good-morning to you both,' says Jack, like an honest fellow as he was. 'If she doesn't marry me except on these conditions, give her my compliments, and tell her our courtship is at an end.'

"But it wasn't long till they soon came out with another story, for before a week passed they were very glad to get him on his own conditions. Jack was now as happy as the day was long—all things appointed for the wedding, and nothing a-wanting to make everything to his heart's content but the wife, and her he was to have in less than no time. For a day or two before the wedding there never was seen such grand preparations: bullocks, and hogs, and sheep were roasted whole—kegs of whisky, both Roscrea and Innishowen, barrels of ale and beer, were there in dozens. All descriptions of niceties, and wild-fowl, and fish from the say, and the dearest wine that could be bought with money, was got for the gentry and grand folks. Fiddlers, and pipers, and harpers—in short, all kinds of music and musicianers played in shoals. Lords and ladies and squares of high degree were present—and, to crown the thing, there was open house for all comers.

"At length the wedding-day arrived; there was nothing but roasting and boiling; servants dressed in rich liveries ran about with joy and delight in their countenances, and white gloves and wedding favours on their hats and hands. To make a long story short, they were all seated in Jack's castle at the wedding breakfast, ready for the priest to marry them when they'd be done; for in them times people were never married until they had laid in a good foundation to carry them through the ceremony. Well, they were all seated round the table, the men dressed in the best of broadcloth, and the ladies rustling in their silks and satins, their heads, necks, and arms hung round with jewels both rich and rare; but of all that were there that day there wasn't the likes of the bride and bridegroom. As for him, nobody could think, at all, at all, that he was ever anything else than a born gintleman; and, what was more to his credit, he had his

123

kind ould mother sitting beside the bride, to tache her that an honest person, though poorly born, is company for the King. As soon as the •breakfast was served up, they all set to, and maybe the vaarious kinds of eatables did not pay for it; and amongst all this cutting and thrusting, no doubt but it was remarked that the bride herself was behindhand wid none of them—that she took her dalin-trick without flinching, and made nothing less than a right fog meal of it; and small blame to her for that same, you persave.

"When the breakfast was over, up gets Father Flanagan, out with his book, and on with his stole, to marry them. The bride and bridegroom went up to the end of the room, attended by their friends, and the rest of the company stood on each side of it; for, you see, they were too high bred, and knew their manners too well, to stand in a crowd like *spalpeens*. For all that, there was many a sly look from the ladies to their bachelors, and many a titter among them, grand as they were; for, to tell the truth, the best of them likes to see fun in the way, particularly of that sort. The priest himself was in as great a glee as any of them, only he kept it under, and well he might, for sure enough this marriage was nothing less than a rale windfall to him, and the parson that was to marry them after him—bekase, you persave, a Protestant and Catholic must be married by both, otherwise it doesn't hould good in law. The parson was as grave as a mustard-pot, and Father Flanagan called the bride and bridegroom his childher, which was a big bounce for him to say the likes of, more betoken that neither of them was a drop's blood to him.

"However, he pulled out the book, and was just be ginning to buckle them, when in comes Jack's ould acquaintance, the smoking cur, as grave as ever. The priest had just got through two or three words of Latin, when the dog gives him a pluck by the sleeve. Father Flanagan, of coorse, turned round to see who it was that nudged him. 'Behave yourself,' says the dog to him, just as he peeped over his shoulder—'behave yourself,' says he; and with that he sot him down on his hunkers beside the priest, and pulling a cigar, instead of a pipe, out of his pocket, he put it in his mouth, and began to smoke for the bare life of him. And, by my own word, it's he that could smoke : at times he would shoot the smoke in a slender stream, like a knitting-needle, with a round curl at the one end of it, ever so far out of the right side of his mouth ; then he would shoot it out of the left, and sometimes make it swirl out so beautiful from the middle of his lips !—why, then, it's he that must have been the well-bred puppy all out, as far as smoking went. Father Flanagan and they all were tundherstruck.

" ' In the name of St. Anthony, and of that holy nun St. Teresa,' said his reverence to him, ' who or what are you, at all, at all ? '

" ' Never mind that,' says the dog, taking the cigar for a minute between his claws; ' but if you wish particularly to know, I'm a thirty-second cousin of your own, by the mother's side.'

" ' I command you, in the name of all the saints,' says Father Flanagan, ' to disappear from among us, and never become visible to any one in this house again.'

" ' The sorra a budge, at the present time, will I budge,' says the dog to him, ' until I see all sides rightified, and the rogues disappointed.'

" Now one would be apt to think the appearance of a spaking dog might be after fright'ning the ladies ; but doesn't all the world know that spaking puppies are their greatest favourites. Instead of that, you see, there was half a dozen of fierce-looking whiskered fellows, and three or four half-pay officers, that were nearer making off than the ladies. But, besides the cigar, the dog had, upon this occasion, a pair of green spectacles acrass his face, and through these, while he was spaking to Father Flanagan, he ogled all the ladies, one after another, and when his eye would light upon any that pleased him he would kiss his paw to her and wag his tail with the greatest politeness.

" ' John,' says Father Flanagan to one of the servants, ' bring me salt and water, till I consecrate them to banish the divil, for he has appeared to us all during broad daylight, in the shape of a dog.'

" ' You had better behave yourself, I say again,' says the dog, ' or if you make me speak, by my honour as a gintleman, I'll expose you. I say, you won't marry the same two, neither this nor any other day, and I'll give you my rasons presently; but I repate it, Father Flanagan, if you compel me to speak, I'll make you look nine ways at once.'

" 'I defy you, Satan,' says the priest; 'and if you don't take yourself away before the holy wather's made, I'll send you off in a flame of fire.'

" 'Yes, I'm trimbling,' says the dog: 'plenty of spirits you laid in your day, but it was in a place that's nearer us than the Red Sea you did it. Listen to me, though, for I don't wish to expose you, as I said.' So he gets on his hind legs, put his nose to the priest's ear, and whispers something to him that none of the rest could hear—all before the priest had time to know where he was. At any rate, whatever he said seemed to make his reverence look double, though, faix, that wasn't hard to do, for he was as big as two common men. When the dog was done speaking, and had put his cigar in his mouth, the priest seemed tundherstruck, crossed himself, and was, no doubt of it, in great perplexity.

" 'I say it's false,' says Father Flanagan, plucking up courage; 'but you know you're a liar, and the father of liars.'

" 'As thrue as gospel, this bout, I tell you,' says the dog.

" 'Wait till I make my holy wather,' says the priest, 'and if I don't cork you in a thumb bottle for this, I'm not here.'

" 'You're better at uncorking,' says the dog—'better at relasing spirits than confining them.'

" Just at this minute the whole company sees a gintleman galloping for the bare life of him up to the hall-door, and he dressed like an officer. In three jiffeys he was down off his horse, and in among the company. The dog, as soon as he made his appearance, laid his claw as usual on his nose, and gave the bridegroom a wink, as much as to say, 'Watch what'll happen.'

" Now it was very odd that Jack, during all this time, remembered the dog very well, but could never once think of the darling that did so much for him. As soon, however, as the officer made his appearance, the bride seemed as if she would sink outright; and when he walked up to her, to ax what was the meaning of what he saw, why, down she drops at once—fainted clane. The gintleman then went up to Jack, and says, 'Sir, was this lady about to be married to you?'

"'Sartinly,' says Jack; 'we were going to be yoked in the blessed and holy tackle of mathrimony,' or some high-flown words of that kind.

"'Well, sir,' says the other back to him, 'I can only say that she is most solemnly sworn never to marry another man but me. That oath she tuck when I was joining my regiment before it went abroad; and if the ceremony of your marriage be performed, you will sleep with a perjured bride.'

"Begad, he did, plump before all their faces. Jack, of coorse, was struck all of a hape at this; but as he had the bride in his arms, giving her a little sup of whisky to bring her to, you persave, he couldn't make him an answer. However, she soon came to herself, and, on opening her eyes, 'Oh! hide me, hide me!' says she, 'for I can't bear to look on him!'

"'He says you are his sworn bride, my darling,' says Jack.

"'I am—I am,' says she, covering her eyes, and crying away at the rate of a wedding. 'I can't deny it; and, by tare-an-ounty!' says she, 'I'm unworthy to be either his wife or yours; for, except I marry you both, I dunna how to settle this affair between you at all—oh, murther *sheery!* but I'm the misfortunate crathur entirely.'

"'Well,' says Jack to the officer, 'nobody can do more than be sorry for a wrong turn; small blame to her for taking a fancy to your humble servant, Mr. Officer'—and he stood as tall as possible, to show himself off. 'You see the fair lady is sorrowful for her folly; so, as it's not yet too late, and as you came in the nick of time, in the name of Providence take my place, and let the marriage go an.'

"'No,' says she, 'never; I'm not worthy of him, at all, at all! Tundher-an-age, but I'm the unlucky thief!'

"While this was going forward, the officer looked closely at Jack, and seeing him such a fine, handsome fellow, and having heard before of his riches, he began to think that, all things considhered, she wasn't so much to be blempt. Then, when he saw how sorry she was for having forgot him, he steps forrid.

127

" ' Well,' says he, ' I'm still willing to marry you, particularly as you feel conthrition——' "

" He should have said contrition, confession, and satisfaction," observed Father Peter.

" Pether, will you keep your theology to yourself," replied Father Ned, "and let us come to the plot without interruption."

"Plot!" exclaimed Father Peter. "I'm sure it's no rebellion, that there should be a plot in it, any way ! "

" *Tace*," said Father Ned—" *tace*, and that's Latin for a candle."

" I deny that," said the curate ; " *tace* is the imperative mood from *taceo*, to keep silent. *Taceo, taces, tacui, tacere, tacendi, tacendo, tac*——"

" Ned, go on with your story, and never mind that deep larning of his—he's almost cracked with it," said the superior : " go on, and never mind him."

" ' Well,' says he, ' I'm still willing to marry you, particularly as you feel conthrition for what you were going to do.' So, with this, they all gother about her, and, as the officer was a fine fellow himself, prevailed upon her to let the marriage be performed, and they were accordingly spliced as fast as his reverence could make them.

" ' Now, Jack,' says the dog, ' I want to spake with you for a minute—it's a word for your own ear.' So he stands up on his two hind legs, and purtinded to be whisp'ring something to him ; but what do you think ?—he gives him the slightest touch on the lips with his paw, and that instant Jack remimbered the lady and everything that happened betune them.

" ' Tell me this instant,' says Jack, seizing him by the throath, ' where's the darling, at all, at all ? '

" Jack spoke finer nor this, to be sure ; but, as I can't give his tall English, the sorra one of me will bother myself striving to do it.

" ' Behave yourself,' says the dog ; ' just say nothing, only follow me.'

" Accordingly, Jack went out with the dog, and in a few minutes comes in again, leading along with him, on the one side, the loveliest lady that ever eye beheld, and the dog, that was her brother, now metamurphied into a beautiful, illegant gintleman, on the other.

"'Father Flanagan,' says Jack, 'you thought a while ago you'd have no marriage, but instead of that you'll have a brace of them;' up and telling the company, at the same time, all that happened him, and how the beautiful crathur that he brought in with him had done so much for him.

"Whin the gintlemen heard this, as they were all Irishmen, you may be sure there was nothing but huzzaing and throwing up of hats from them, and waving of hankerchers from the ladies. Well, my dear, the wedding dinner was ate in great style; the nobleman promised no disgrace to his rank at the trencher; and so, to make a long story short, such faisting and banqueteering was never seen since or before. At last night came; and, among ourselves, not a doubt of it, but Jack thought himself a happy man; and, maybe, if all was known, the bride was much of the same opinion: be that as it may, night came—the bride, all blushing, beautiful, and modest as your own sweetheart, was getting tired after the dancing; Jack, too, though much stouter, wished for a trifle of repose, and many thought it was near time to throw the stocking, as is proper, of coorse, on every occasion of the kind. Well, he was just on his way upstairs, and had reached the first landing, when he hears a voice at his ear shouting, 'Jack, Jack—Jack Magennis!' Jack could have spitted anybody for coming to disturb him at such a criticality. 'Jack Magennis!' says the voice. Jack looked about to see who it was that called him, and there he found himself lying on the green Rath, a little above his mother's cabin, of a fine calm summer's evening in the month of June. His mother was stooping over him, with her mouth at his ear, striving to waken him by shouting and shaking him out of his sleep.

"'Oh! by this and by that, mother,' says Jack, 'what did you waken me for?'

"'Jack, *avourneen*,' says the mother, 'sure and you war lying grunting, and groaning, and snifthering there, for all the world as if you had the colic; and I only nudged you for fraid you war in pain.'

"'I wouldn't for a thousand guineas,' says Jack, 'that ever you wakened me, at all, at all; but whisht, mother, go into the house, and I'll be afther you in less than no time.'

"The mother went in, and the first thing Jack did was

to try the rock, and, sure enough, there he found as much money as made him the richest man that ever was in the country. And what was to his credit, when he did grow rich he wouldn't let his cabin be thrown down, but built a fine castle on a spot near it, where he could always have it under his eye, to prevent him from getting proud. In the coorse of time, a harper, hearing the story, composed a tune upon it which everybody knows is called the 'Little House under the Hill' to this day, beginning with—

'Hi for it, ho for it, hi for it still;
Och, and whoo! your sowl—hi for the little house under the hill!'.

"So you see that was the way the great Magennises first came by their wealth, and all because Jack was industrious, and an obadient, dutiful, tindher son to his helpless ould mother; and well he desarved what he got, *ershi misha*.[1] Your healths—Father Ned—Father Pether—all kinds of happiness to us; and there's my story."

"Well," said Father Peter, "I think that dog was nothing more or less than a downright cur, that deserved the lash nine times a day, if it was only for his want of respect to the clergy; if he had given me such insolence, I solemnly declare I would have bate the devil out of him with a hazel cudgel, if I failed to exorcise him with a prayer."

Father Ned looked at the simple and credulous curate with an expression of humour and astonishment.

"Paddy," said he to the servant, "will you let us know what the night's doing?"

Paddy looked out. "Why, your rev'rence, it's a fine night, all out, and cleared up it is bravely."

At this moment the stranger awoke. "Sir," said Father Ned, "you missed an amusing story in consequence of your somnolency."

"Though I missed the story," replied the stranger, "I was happy enough to hear your friend's critique upon the dog."

Father Ned seemed embarrassed. The curate, on the contrary, exclaimed with triumph, "But wasn't I right, sir?"

Say I.

"Perfectly," said the stranger; "the moral you applied was excellent."

"Good-night, boys," said Father Ned—"good-night, Mr. Longinus Polysyllabus Alexandrinus!"

"Good-night, boys," said Father Peter, imitating Father Ned, whom he looked upon as a perfect model of courtesy—"good-night, boys; good-night, Mr. Longinus Polysyllabus Alexandrinus!"

"Good-night," replied the stranger; "good-night, Doctor Ned—hem!—Doctor Edward Deleery; and good-night, Dr. Peter M'Clatchaghan—good-night!"

When the clergymen were gone, the circle about the fire, excepting the members of Ned's family and the stranger, dispersed to their respective homes; and thus ended the amusement of that evening.

After they had separated, Ned, whose curiosity respecting the stranger was by no means satisfied, began to sift him in his own peculiar manner as they both sat at the fire.

"Well, sir," said Ned, "barring the long playacther that tumbles upon the big stage in the street of our market-town here below, I haven't seen so long a man this many a day; and, barring your big whiskers, the sorra one of your honour's unlike him. A fine portly vagabone he is, indeed—a big man; and a bigger rogue, they say, for he pays nobody."

"Have you got such a company in your neighbourhood?" inquired the stranger, with indifference.

"We have, sir," said Ned; "but, plase goodness, they'll soon be lashed like hounds from the place—the town boys are preparing to give them a chivey some fine morning out of the country."

"Indeed!—he—hem!—that will be very spirited of the town boys," said the stranger dryly.

"That's a smart-looking horse your honour rides," observed Ned; "did he carry you far to-day, with submission?"

"Not far," replied his companion—"only fourteen miles. But, I suppose, the fact is, you wish to know who and what I am, where I came from, and whither I am going. Well, you shall know this. In the first place, I am agent to Lord Non-Resident's estate, if you ever heard of that nobleman,

131

and I am on my way from Castle Ruin, the seat of his lordship's encumbrances, to Dublin. My name you have already heard. Are you now satisfied?"

"Parfitly, your honour," replied Ned, "and I'm much obliged to you, sir."

"I trust you are an honest man," said the stranger; "because, for this night, I am about to place great confidence in you."

"Well, sir," said his landlord, "if I turn out dishonest to you, it's more nor I did in my whole life to anybody else, barring to Nancy."

"Here, then," said the stranger, drawing out a large packet, enclosed in a roll of black leather, "here is the half-year's rent of the estate, together with my own property; keep it secure till morning, when I shall demand it, and, of course, it will be safe?"

"As if it was five fadom under ground," replied Ned. "I will put it along with our own trifle of silver; and after that, let Nancy alone for keeping it safe so long as it's there!" saying which, Ned secured the packet, and showed the stranger his bed.

About five o'clock the next morning their guest was up, and ordered a snack in all haste. "Being a military man," said he, "and accustomed to timely hours, I shall ride down to the town, and put a letter into the post-office in time for the Dublin mail, after which you may expect me to breakfast. But, in the meantime, I am not to go with empty pockets," he added, when mounting his horse at the door. "Bring me silver, landlord, and be quick."

"How much, plase your honour?"

"Twenty or thirty shillings; but, harkee, produce my packet, that I may be certain my property is safe."

"Here it is, your honour, safe and sound," replied Ned; "and Nancy, sir, has sent you all the silver she has, which was one pound five; but I'd take it as a favour if your honour would be contint with twenty shillings, and lave me the other five; for you see the case is this, sir, plase your honour, she"—and Ned, with a shrewd humorous nod, pointed with his thumb over his shoulder as he spoke—"she wears the— what you know, sir."

132

"Ay, I thought so," replied the stranger; "but a man of your size, to be hen-pecked, must be a great knave, otherwise your wife would allow you more liberty. Go in, man; you deserve no compassion in such an age of freedom as this. I shan't give you a farthing till after my return, and only then if it be agreeable to your wife."

"Murdher!" said Ned, astonished. "I beg your honour's pardon; murdher alive, sir, where's your whiskers?"

The stranger put his hand hastily to his face, and smiled. "Where are my whiskers? Why, shaved off, to be sure," he replied; and setting spurs to his horse, was soon out of sight and hearing.

It was nearly a month after that when Ned and Nancy, in presence of Father Deleery, opened the packet, and discovered, not the half year's rent of Lord Non-Resident's estate, but a large sheaf of play-bills packed up together—their guest having been the identical person to whom Ned affirmed he bore so strong a resemblance.

AN ESSAY ON IRISH SWEARING

NO pen can do justice to the extravagance and frolic inseparable from the character of the Irish people; nor has any system of philosophy been discovered that can with moral fitness be applied to them. Phrenology fails to explain it, for, according to the most capital surveys hitherto made and reported on, it appears that, inasmuch as the moral and intellectual organs of Irishmen predominate over the physical and sensual, the people ought therefore to be ranked at the very tip-top of morality. We would warn the phrenologists, however, not to be too sanguine in drawing inferences from an examination of Paddy's head. Heaven only knows the scenes in which it is engaged, and the protuberances created by a long life of hard fighting. Many an organ and development is brought out on it by the cudgel, that never would have appeared had Nature been left to herself.

Drinking, fighting, and swearing are the three great characteristics of every people. Paddy's love of fighting and of whisky has been long proverbial; and of his tact in swearing much has also been said. But there is one department of oath-making in which he stands unrivalled and unapproachable: I mean the *alibi*. There is where he shines, where his oath, instead of being a mere matter of fact or opinion, rises up into the dignity of epic narrative, containing within itself all the complexity of machinery, harmony of parts, and fertility of invention by which your true epic should be characterised.

The Englishman, whom we will call the historian in swearing, will depose to the truth of this or that fact, but there the line is drawn: he swears his oath so far as he knows, and stands still. "I'm sure, for my part, I don't know; I've said all I knows about it," and beyond this his besotted intellect goeth not.

The Scotchman, on the other hand, who is the metaphysician in swearing, sometimes borders on equivocation. He decidedly goes further than the Englishman, not because he has less honesty, but more prudence. He will assent to, or deny, a proposition; for the Englishman's "I don't know," and the Scotchman's "I dinna ken," are two very distinct assertions when properly understood. The former stands out a monument of dulness, an insuperable barrier against inquiry, ingenuity, and fancy; but the latter frequently stretches itself so as to embrace hypothetically a particular opinion.

But Paddy!—put him forward to prove an *alibi* for his four-teenth or fifteenth cousin, and you will be gratified by the pomp, pride, and circumstance of true swearing. Every oath with him is an epic—pure poetry, abounding with humour, pathos, and the highest order of invention and talent. He is not at ease, it is true, under facts; there is something too commonplace in dealing with them, which his genius scorns. But his flights —his flights are beautiful; and his episodes admirable and happy. In fact, he is an *improvisatore* at oath-taking, with this difference, that his *extempore* oaths possess all the ease and correctness of labour and design.

He is not, however, altogether averse to facts; but, like your true poet, he veils, changes, and modifies them with such skill that they possess all the merit and graces of fiction. If he happen to make an assertion incompatible with the plan of the piece, his genius acquires fresh energy, enables him to widen the design, and to create new machinery, with such happiness of adaptation that what appeared out of proportion or character is made in his hands to contribute to the general strength and beauty of the oath.

· 'Tis true there is nothing perfect under the sun; but if there were, it would certainly be Paddy at an *alibi*. Some flaws no doubt occur, some slight inaccuracies may be noticed by a critical eye, an occasional anachronism stands out, and a mistake or so in geography; but let it be recollected that Paddy's *alibi* is but a human production, let us not judge him by harsher rules than those which we apply to Homer, Virgil, or Shakespeare.

Aliquando bonus dormitat Homerus is allowed on all hands. Virgil made Dido and Æneas contemporary, though they were not so; and Shakespeare, by the creative power of his genius, changed an inland town into a sea-port. Come, come, have bowels. Let epic swearing be treated with the same courtesy shown to epic poetry, that is if both are the production of a rare genius. I maintain that when Paddy commits a blemish he is too harshly admonished for it. When he soars out of sight here, as occasionally happens, does he not frequently alight somewhere about Sydney Bay, much against his own inclination? And if he puts forth a hasty production, is he not compelled for the space of seven or fourteen years to revise his oath? But, indeed, few works of fiction are properly encouraged in Ireland.

It would be unpardonable in us, however, to overlook the beneficial effects of Paddy's peculiar genius in swearing *alibis*. Some persons, who display their own egregious ignorance of morality, may be disposed to think that it tends to lessen the obligation of an oath by inducing a habit among the people of swearing to what is not true. We look upon such persons as very dangerous to Ireland and to the repeal of the Union, and we request them not to push their principles too far in the disturbed parts of the country. Could society hold together a single day if nothing but truth were spoken? Would not law and lawyers soon become obsolete if nothing but truth were sworn? What would become of Parliament if truth alone were uttered there? Its annual proceedings might be despatched in a month. Fiction is the basis of society, the bond of commercial prosperity, the channel of communication between nation and nation, and not unfrequently the interpreter between a man and his own conscience.

For these and many other reasons which we could adduce, we say with Paddy, "Long life to fiction!" When associated with swearing it shines in its brightest colours. What, for instance, is calculated to produce the best and purest of the moral virtues so beautifully as the swearing an *alibi?* Here are fortitude and a love of freedom resisting oppression; for it is well known that all law is oppression in Ireland.

There is compassion for the peculiar state of the poor boy who perhaps only burnt a family in their beds; benevolence to prompt the generous effort in his behalf; disinterestedness to run the risk of becoming an involuntary absentee; fortitude in encountering a host of brazen-faced lawyers; patience under

136

the unsparing gripe of a cross-examiner; perseverance in conducting the oath to its close against a host of difficulties; and friendship, which bottoms and crowns them all.

Paddy's merits, however, touching the *alibi*, rest not here. Fiction on these occasions only teaches him how to perform a duty. It may be that he is under the obligation of a previous oath not to give evidence against certain of his friends and associates. Now, could anything in the whole circle of religion or ethics be conceived that renders the epic style of swearing so incumbent upon Paddy? There is a kind of moral fitness in all things; for where the necessity of invention exists, it is consolatory to reflect that the ability to invent is bestowed along with it.

Next to the *alibi* come Paddy's powers in sustaining a cross-examination. Many persons think that this is his *forte ;* but we cannot yield to such an opinion, nor compromise his originality of conception in the scope and plan of an *alibi*. It is marked by a minuteness of touch and a peculiarity of expression which give it every appearance of real life. The circumstances are so well imagined, the groups so naturally disposed, the colouring so finished, and the background in such fine perspective, that the whole picture presents you with such keeping and *vraisemblance* as could be accomplished only by the genius of a master.

In point of interest, however, we must admit that his ability in a cross-examination ranks next to his skill in planning an *alibi*. There is in the former a versatility of talent that keeps him always ready; a happiness of retort, generally disastrous to the wit of the most established cross-examiner; an apparent simplicity which is quite as impenetrable as the lawyer's assurance; a *vis comica* which puts the court in tears; and an originality of sorrow that often convulses it with laughter. His resources, when he is pressed, are inexhaustible; and the address with which he contrives to gain time, that he may suit his reply to the object of his evidence, is beyond all praise. And yet his appearance when he mounts the table is anything but prepossessing; a sheepish look, and a loose-jointed frame of body, wrapped in a frieze greatcoat, do not promise much. Nay, there is often a rueful, blank expression in his visage which might lead a stranger to anticipate nothing but

137

blunders and dulness. This, however, is hypocrisy of the first water. Just observe the tact with which he places his *caubeen* upon the table, his *kippeen* across it, and the experienced air with which he pulls up the waistband of his breeches, absolutely girding his loins for battle. 'Tis true his blue eye has at present nothing remarkable in it except a drop or two of the native; but that is not remarkable.

When the direct examination has been concluded, nothing can be finer than the simplicity with which he turns round to the lawyer who is to cross-examine him. Yet, as if conscious that firmness and caution are his main guards, he again pulls up his waistband with a more vigorous hitch, looks shyly into the very eyes of his opponent, and awaits the first blow.

The question at length comes; and Paddy, after having raised the collar of his big coat on his shoulder, and twisted up the shoulder along with it, directly puts the query back to the lawyer, without altering a syllable of it, for the purpose of ascertaining more accurately whether that is the precise question that has been put to him; for Paddy is conscientious. Then is the science displayed on both sides. The one a veteran, trained in all the technicalities of legal puzzles, irony, blarney, sarcasm, impudence, stock jokes, quirks, rigmarolery, brow-beating, ridicule, and subtlety; the other a poor peasant, relying only upon the justice of a good cause and the gifts of nature, without either experience or learning, and with nothing but his native modesty to meet the forensic effrontery of his antagonist.

Our readers will perceive that the odds are a thousand to one against Paddy; yet, when he replies to a hackneyed genius at cross-examination, how does it happen that he uniformly elicits those roars of laughter which rise in the court, and convulse it from the judge to the crier? In this laugh, which is usually at the expense of the cross-examiner, Paddy himself always joins, so that the counsel has the double satisfaction of being made not only the jest of the judge and his brother lawyers, but of the ragged witness whom he attempted to make ridiculous.

It is not impossible that this merry mode of dispensing justice may somewhat encourage Paddy in that independence of mind which relishes not the idea of being altogether bound by oaths that are too often administered with a jocular spirit. To many of the uninitiated Irish an oath is a solemn, to some an awful thing. Of this wholesome reverence for its sanction, two or three testimonies given in a court of justice usually cure them. The indifferent, business-like manner in which the oaths are put, the sing-song tone of voice, the rapid utterance of the words, give to this solemn act an appearance of excellent burlesque, which ultimately renders the whole proceedings remarkable for the absence of truth and reality; but, at the same time, gives them unquestionable merit as a dramatic representation, abounding with fiction, well related, and ably acted.

Thumb-kissing is another feature in Paddy's adroitness too important to be passed over in silence. Here his tact shines out again. It would be impossible for him in many cases to meet the perplexities of a cross-examination so cleverly as he does, if he did not believe that he had, by kissing his thumb instead of the book, actually taken no oath, and consequently given to himself a wider range of action. We must admit, however, that this very circumstance involves him in difficulties which are sometimes peculiarly embarrassing. Taking everything into consideration, the prospect of freedom for his sixth cousin, the consciousness of having kissed his thumb, or the consoling reflection that he swore only on a " Law " Bible, it must be granted that the opportunities presented by a cross-examination are well calculated to display his wit, humour, and fertility of invention. He is accordingly great in it; but still we maintain that his execution of an *alibi* is his ablest performance, comprising, as it does, both the conception and construction of the work.

Both the oaths and imprecations of the Irish display, like those who use them, indications of great cruelty and great humour. Many of the former exhibit that ingenuity which comes out when Paddy is on his cross-examination in a court of justice. Every people, it is true, have resorted to the habit of mutilating or changing in their oaths the letters which form the Creator's name; but we question if any have surpassed the Irish in the cleverness with which they accomplish it. Mock oaths are habitual to Irishmen in ordinary conversation; but the use of any [or all of them is not considered to constitute an oath; on the contrary, they are in the mouths of many who would not, except upon a very solemn occasion indeed, swear by the name of the Deity in its proper form.

The ingenuity of their mock oaths is sufficient to occasion much perplexity to any one disposed to consider it in connection with the character and moral feelings of the people. Whether to note it as a reluctance on their part to incur the guilt of an oath, or as a proof of habitual tact in evading it by artifice, is manifestly a difficulty hard to be overcome. We are decidedly inclined to the former; for although there is much laxity of principle among Irishmen, naturally to be expected from men whose moral state has been neglected by the legislature, and deteriorated by political and religious asperity, acting upon quick passions and badly-regulated minds—yet we know that they possess, after all, a strong but vague, undirected sense of devotional feeling and reverence, which are associated with great crimes and dark shades of character. This explains one chief cause of the sympathy which is felt in Ireland for criminals from whom the law exacts the fatal penalty of death; and it also accounts, independently of the existence of any illegal association, for the terrible retribution inflicted upon those who come forward to prosecute them. It is not in Ireland with criminals as in other countries, where the character of a murderer or incendiary is notoriously bad, as resulting from a life of gradual profligacy and villainy. Far from it. In Ireland you will find those crimes perpetrated by men who are good fathers, good husbands, good sons, and good neighbours—by men who would share their last morsel or their last shilling with a fellow-creature in distress—who would generously lose their lives for a man who had obliged them, provided he had not incurred their enmity—and who would protect a defenceless stranger as far as lay in their power.

There are some mock oaths among Irishmen which must have had their origin amongst those whose habits of thought were much more elevated than could be supposed to characterise the lower orders. "By the powers of death" is never now used as we have written it; but the ludicrous travesty of it, "By the powdhers o' delf," is quite common. Of this and other mock oaths it may be right to observe that those who swear by them are in general ignorant of their proper origin. There are some, however, of this description whose original form is well known. One of these Paddy displays considerable ingenuity in using. "By the cross" can scarcely be classed under the mock oaths; but the manner in which it is pressed into asseverations is amusing. When Paddy is affirming a truth he swears "by the crass" simply, and this with him is an oath of considerable obligation. He generally, in order to render it more impressive, accompanies it with suitable action, that is, he places the forefinger of each hand across, that he may assail you through two senses instead of one. On the contrary, when he intends to hoax you by asserting what is not true, he ingeniously multiplies the oath, and swears "by the five crasses," that is, by his own five fingers, placing at the same time his four fingers and his thumbs across each other in a most impressive and vehement manner. Don't believe him then—the knave is lying as fast as possible, and with no remorse. "By the crass o' Christ" is an oath of much solemnity, and seldom used in a falsehood. Paddy also often places two bits of straw across, and sometimes two sticks, upon which he swears with an appearance of great heat and sincerity—*sed caveto.*

Irishmen generally consider iron as a sacred metal. In the interior of the country the thieves (but few in number) are frequently averse to stealing it. Why it possesses this hold upon their affections it is difficult to say, but it is certain that they rank it among their sacred things; consider that to find it is lucky, and nail it over their doors when found in the convenient shape of a horseshoe. It is also used as a medium of asserting truth. We believe, however, that the sanction it imposes is not very strong. "By this blessed iron!" "By this blessed an' holy iron!" are oaths of an inferior grade; but if the circumstance on which they are founded be a matter of indifference, they seldom depart from truth in using them.

Paddy, when engaged in a fight, is never at a loss for a weapon, and we may also affirm that he is never at a loss for an oath. When relating a narrative, or some other circum-

stance of his own invention, if contradicted, he will corrobo-
rate it, in order to sustain his credit or produce the proper
impression, by an abrupt oath upon the first object he can
seize. "*Arrah*, nonsense! by this pipe in my hand, it's as
thrue as"—and then, before he completes the illustration, he
goes on with a fine specimen of equivocation—"By the stool
I'm sittin' an, it is; an' what more would you have from me,
barrin' I take my book oath of it?" Thus does he, under
the mask of an insinuation, induce you to believe that he has
actually sworn it, whereas the oath is always left undefined
and incomplete.

Sometimes he is exceedingly comprehensive in his adjura-
tions, and swears upon a magnificent scale; as, for instance,
"By the contints of all the books that ever wor opened an'
shut, it's as thrue as the sun to the dial." This certainly
leaves "the five crasses" immeasurably behind. However,
be cautious, and not too confident in taking so sweeping and
learned an oath upon trust, notwithstanding its imposing
effect. We grant, indeed, that an oath which comprehends
within its scope all the learned libraries of Europe, including
even the Alexandrian of old, is not only an erudite one, but
establishes in a high degree the taste of the swearer, and displays on his part an uncommon grasp of intellect. Still we
recommend you, whenever you hear an alleged fact substan-
tiated by it, to set your ear as sharply as possible; for, after
all, it is more than probable that every book by which he has
sworn might be contained in a nutshell. The secret may be
briefly explained. Paddy is in the habit of substituting the
word never for ever. "By all the books that never were
opened or shut," the reader perceives, is only a flourish of
trumpets—a mere delusion of the enemy.

In fact, Paddy has oaths rising gradually from the lying
ludicrous to the superstitious solemn, each of which finely
illustrates the nature of the subject to which it is applied.
When he swears "by the contints o' Moll Kelly's Primer," or
"by the piper that played afore Moses," you are perhaps as
strongly inclined to believe him as when he draws upon a
more serious oath—that is, you almost regret the thing is
not the gospel that Paddy asserts it to be. In the former
sense, the humorous narrative which calls forth the laughable

burlseque of "by the piper o' Moses," is usually the richest lie in the whole range of fiction.

Paddy is, in his ejaculatory as well as in all his other mock oaths, a kind of smuggler in morality, imposing as often as he can upon his own conscience, and upon those who exercise spiritual authority over him. Perhaps more of his oaths are blood-stained than would be found among the inhabitants of all Christendom put together.

Paddy's oaths in his amours are generally rich specimens of humorous knavery and cunning. It occasionally happens— but for the honour of our virtuous countrywomen, we say but rarely—that by the honey of his flattering and delusive tongue he succeeds in placing some unsuspecting girl's reputation in rather a hazardous predicament. When the priest comes to investigate the affair, and to cause him to make compensation to the innocent creature who suffered by his blandishments, it is almost uniformly ascertained that, in order to satisfy her scruples as to the honesty of his promises, he had sworn marriage to her on a book of ballads ! ! ! In other cases blank books have been used for the same purpose.

If, however, you wish to pin Paddy up in a corner, get him a relic, a Catholic prayer-book, or a Douay Bible to swear upon. Here is where the fox—notwithstanding all his turnings and windings upon heretic Bibles, books of ballads, or mock oaths—is caught at last. The strongest principle in him is superstition. It may be found as the prime mover in his best and worst actions. An atrocious man who is superstitious, will perform many good and charitable actions, with a hope that their merit in the sight of God may cancel the guilt of his crimes. On the other hand, a good man who is superstitiously the slave of his religious opinions, will lend himself to those illegal combinations whose object is, by keeping ready a system of organised opposition to an heretical government, to fulfil, if a political crisis should render it practicable, the absurd prophecies of Pastorini[1] and Columbkill.[2]

---

[1] Pastorini was an Italian writer whose history of the Christian Church "past and future," as indicated in prophecy, was translated about 1810, and became immensely popular in Ireland.—ED.

[2] Some forgeries concocted, we are told, by order of the English Government, as one of the means of subduing the people. For a couple of centuries the people implicitly believed in them.—ED.

Although the prophecies of the former would appear to be out of date to a rational reader, yet Paddy, who can see farther into prophecy than any rational reader, honestly believes that Pastorini has left, for those who are superstitiously given, sufficient range of expectation in several parts of his work.

We might enumerate many other oaths in frequent use among the peasantry; but, as our object is not to detail them at full length, we trust that those already specified may be considered sufficient to enable our readers to get a fuller insight into their character and their moral influence upon the people.

The next thing which occurs to us in connection with the present subject is cursing; and here again Paddy holds the first place. His imprecations are often full, bitter, and intense. Indeed, there is more poetry and epigrammatic point in them than in those of any other country in the world.

We find it a difficult thing to enumerate the Irish curses so as to do justice to a subject so varied and so liable to be shifted and improved by the fertile genius of those who send them abroad. Indeed, to reduce them into order and method would be a task of considerable difficulty. Every occasion and every fit of passion frequently produce a new curse, perhaps equal in bitterness to any that has gone before it.

Many of the Irish imprecations are difficult to be understood, having their origin in some historical event, or in poetical metaphors that require a considerable process of reasoning to explain them. Of this twofold class is that general one—"The curse of Cromwell on you!" which means, "May you suffer all that a tyrant like Cromwell would inflict!" and "The curse o' the crows upon you!" which is probably an allusion to the Danish invasion, a raven being the symbol of Denmark; or it may be tantamount to "May you rot on the hills, that the crows may feed upon your carcass!" Perhaps it may thus be understood to imprecate death upon you or some member of your house—alluding to the superstition of rooks hovering over the habitations of the sick, when the malady with which they are afflicted is known to be fatal. Indeed, the latter must certainly be the meaning of it, as is evident from the proverb of "Die, an' give the crow a puddin'."

144

"Hell's cure to you!" "The divil's luck to you!" "High hanging to you!" "Hard feeding to you!" "A short coorse to you!" are all pretty intense, and generally used under provocation and passion. In these cases the curses just mentioned are directed immediately to the offensive object, and there certainly is no want of the *malus animus* to give them energy. It would be easy to multiply the imprecations belonging to this class among the peasantry, but the task is rather unpleasant. There are a few, however, which in consequence of their ingenuity we cannot pass over; they are, in sooth, studies for the swearer. "May you never die till you see your own funeral!" is a very beautiful specimen of the periphrasis: it simply means, may you be hanged; for he who is hanged is humorously said to be favoured with a view of that sombre spectacle, by which they mean the crowd that attends an execution. To the same purpose is "May you die wid a caper in your heel!" "May you die in your pumps!" "May your last dance be a hornpipe on the air!" These are all emblematic of hanging, and are uttered sometimes in jest, and occasionally in earnest. "May the grass grow before your door!" is highly imaginative and poetical. Nothing, indeed, can present the mind with a stronger or more picturesque emblem of desolation and ruin. Its malignity is terrible.

There are also mock imprecations as well as mock oaths. Of this character are "The divil go with you and sixpence, an' thin you'll want neither money nor company!" This humorous and considerate curse is generally confined to the female sex. When Paddy happens to be in a romping mood, and teases his sweetheart too much, she usually utters it with a countenance combating with smiles and frowns, whilst she stands in the act of pinning up her dishevelled hair, her cheeks, particularly the one next Paddy, deepened into a becoming blush.

"Bad scran to you!" is another form seldom used in anger; it is the same as "Hard feeding to you!" "Bad win' to you!" is "Ill health to you!" it is nearly the same as "Consumin' (consumption) to you!" Two other imprecations come under this head, which we will class together because they are counterparts of each other, with this difference, that one of them is the most subtilely and intensely withering in its purport that can well be conceived. The one is that common curse, "Bad 'cess to you!" that is, bad success to you; we may identify it with "Hard fortune to you!" The other is a keen one indeed—"Sweet bad luck to you!" Now, whether we consider the epithet sweet as bitterly ironical, or deem it as a wish that prosperity may harden the heart to the accomplishment of future damnation, as in the case of Dives, we must in either sense grant that it is an oath of powerful hatred and venom. Occasionally the curse of "Bad luck to you!" produces an admirable retort, which is pretty common. When one man applies it to another, he is answered with "Good luck to you, thin; but may neither of them ever happen!"

"Six eggs to you, an' half a dozen o' them rotten!" like "The divil go with you an' sixpence!" is another of those pleasantries which mostly occur in the good-humoured *badinage* between the sexes. It implies disappointment.

There is a species of imprecation prevalent among Irishmen which we may term neutral. It is ended by the word bit, and merely results from a habit of swearing where there is no malignity of purpose. An Irishman, when corroborating an assertion, however true or false, will often say, "Bad luck to the bit but it is!" "Divil fire the bit but it's thruth!" "Damn the bit but it is!" and so on. In this form the mind is not moved, nor the passions excited; it is therefore probably the most insipid of all their imprecations.

Some of the most dreadful maledictions are to be heard among the confirmed mendicants of Ireland. The wit, the gall, and the poetry of these are uncommon. "May you melt off the earth like snow off the ditch!" is one of a high order and intense malignity; but it is not exclusively confined to mendicants, although they form that class among which it is most prevalent. Nearly related to this is "May you melt like butther before a summer sun!" These are, indeed, essentially poetical: they present the mind with appropriate imagery, and exhibit a comparison perfectly just and striking, The former we think unrivalled.

Some of the Irish imprecations would appear to have come down to us from the Ordeals. Of this class, probably, are the following: "May this be poison to me!" "May I be roasted on red-hot iron!" Others of them, from their boldness of metaphor, seem to be of Oriental descent. One expression, indeed, is strikingly so. When a deep offence is offered to an Irishman, under such peculiar circumstances that he cannot immediately retaliate, he usually replies to his enemy, "You'll sup sorrow for this!" "You'll curse the day it happened!" "I'll make you rub your heels together!" All these figurative denunciations are used for the purpose of intimating the pain and agony he will compel his enemy to suffer.

We cannot omit a form of imprecation for good, which is also habitual among the peasantry of Ireland. It is certainly harmless, and argues benevolence of heart. We mean such expressions as the following: "Salvation to me!" "May I never do harm!" "May I never do an ill turn!" "May I never sin!" These are generally used by men who are blameless and peaceable in their lives— simple and well disposed in their intercourse with the world.

Next in order are the curses of pilgrims, mendicants, and idiots. Of those also Paddy entertains a wholesome dread— a circumstance which the pilgrim and mendicant turn with great judgment to their own account. Many a legend and anecdote do such chroniclers relate when the family with whom they rest for the night are all seated around the winter hearth. These are often illustrative of the baneful effects of the poor man's curse. Of course, they produce a proper impression; and accordingly Paddy avoids offending such persons in any way that might bring him under their displeasure.

A certain class of curses much dreaded in Ireland are those of the widow and the orphan. There is, however, something touching and beautiful in this fear of injuring the sorrowful and unprotected. It is, we are happy to say, a becoming and prominent feature in Paddy's character; for, to do him justice in his virtues as well as in his vices, we repeat that he cannot be surpassed in his humanity to the lonely widow and her helpless orphans. He will collect a number of his friends, and proceed with them in a body

147

to plant her bit of potato ground, to reap her oats, to draw home her turf, or secure her hay. Nay, he will beguile her of her sorrows with a natural sympathy and delicacy that do him honour; his heart is open to her complaints, and his hand ever extended to assist her.

There is a strange opinion to be found in Ireland upon the subject of curses. The peasantry think that a curse, no matter how uttered, will fall on something, but that it depends upon the person against whom it is directed whether or not it will descend on him. A curse, we have heard them say, will rest for seven years in the air, ready to alight upon the head of the person who provoked the malediction. It hovers over him, like a kite over its prey, watching the moment when he may be abandoned by his guardian angel; if this occurs, it shoots with the rapidity of a meteor on his head, and clings to him in the shape of illness, temptation, or some other calamity.

They think, however, that the blessing of one person may cancel the curse of another; but this opinion does not affect the theory we have just mentioned. When a man experiences an unpleasant accident they will say, "He has had some poor body's curse;" and, on the contrary, when he narrowly escapes it they say, "He has had some poor body's blessing."

There is no country in which the phrases of goodwill and affection are so strong as in Ireland. The Irish language actually flows with the milk and honey of love and friendship. Sweet and palatable is it to the other sex, and sweetly can Paddy, with his deluding ways, administer it to them from the top of his mellifluous tongue, as a dove feeds her young, or as a kind mother her babe, shaping with her own pretty mouth every morsel of the delicate viands before it goes into that of the infant. In this manner does Paddy, seated behind a ditch, of a bright Sunday, when he ought to be at mass, feed up some innocent girl, not with "false music," but with sweet words, for nothing more musical or melting than his brogue ever dissolved a female heart. Indeed, it is of the danger to be apprehended from the melody of his voice that the admirable and appropriate proverb speaks; for, when he addresses his sweetheart under circumstances that justify suspicion, it is generally said, "Paddy's feedin' her up wid false music."

What language has a phrase equal in beauty and tenderness to *cushla machree*—the pulse of my heart? Can it be paralleled in the whole range of all that are, ever were, or ever will be spoken, for music, sweetness, and a knowledge of anatomy? If Paddy is unrivalled at swearing, he fairly throws the world behind him at the blarney. In professing friendship and making love, give him but a taste of the native, and he is a walking honeycomb, that every woman who sees him wishes to have a lick at; and heaven knows that frequently, at all times, and in all places, does he get himself licked on their account.

Another expression of peculiar force is *vick machree*—or, son of my heart. This is not only elegant, but affectionate beyond almost any other phrase except the foregoing. It is, in a sense, somewhat different from that in which the philosophical poet has used it, a beautiful comment upon the sentiment of "the child's the father of the man," uttered by Wordsworth.

We have seen many a youth, on more occasions than one, standing in profound affliction over the dead body of his aged father, exclaiming, "*Ahir, vick machree—vick machree—wuil thu marra wo'um? Wuil thu marra wo'um?*" "Father, son of my heart, son of my heart, art thou dead from me—art thou dead from me?"—an expression, we think, under any circumstances, not to be surpassed in the intensity of domestic affliction which it expresses; but, under those alluded to, we consider it altogether elevated in exquisite and poetic beauty above the most powerful symbols of Oriental imagery.

A third phrase peculiar to love and affection is *Manim asthee hu*—or, "My soul's within you." Every person acquainted with languages knows how much an idiom suffers by a literal translation. How beautiful, then, how tender and powerful, must those short expressions be, uttered, too, with a fervour of manner peculiar to a deeply-feeling people, when, even after a literal translation, they carry so much of their tenderness and energy into a language whose genius is cold when compared to the glowing beauty of the Irish.

Mavourneen dheelish, too, is only a short phrase, but coming warm and mellowed from Paddy's lips into the ear of his *colleen dhas,* it is a perfect spell—a sweet murmur to which the *lenis susurrus* of the Hybla bees is, with all their honey, jarring discord. How tame is "My sweet darling," its literal translation, compared to its soft and lulling intonations. There is a dissolving, entrancing, beguiling, deluding, flattering, insinuating, coaxing, winning, inveigling, roguish, palavering, come-over-ing, comedhering, consenting, blarneying, killing, willing, charm in it, worth all the philtres that ever the gross knavery of a withered alchymist imposed upon the credulity of those who inhabit the other nations of the earth—for we don't read that these shrivelled philtre-mongers ever prospered in Ireland.

No, no—let Paddy alone. If he hates intensely, effectually, and *inquestingly,* he loves intensely, comprehensively, and gallantly. To love with power is a proof of a large soul; and to hate well is, according to the great moralist, a thing in itself to be loved. Ireland is, therefore, through all its sects, parties, and religions, an amicable nation. Their affections are indeed so vivid that they scruple not to kill each other with kindness; and we very much fear that the march of love and murder will not only keep pace with, but outstrip, the march of intellect.